Mrs F. Brown
3 Larch Way
Longridge, Preston
Lancs PR3 3HF
Tel. 01772 783508

AUTUMN PRELUDE

Felicity Brown

Pen Press

AUTUMN PRELUDE is the first story to emerge from a large box of writings by Felicity Brown, the earliest being a pony book started when she was seventeen. She has had many jobs including three years in London temping and in the Civil Service. A widow now and retired from thirty years of book-keeping for the family firm, she divides her time, when not writing, between entertaining her loved ones, lunching out with friends, painting in oils and doing crosswords and Sudokas, to which she is addicted. She lives in Lancashire on the edge of the Forest of Bowland and has two married children and five grandchildren.

First published in Great Britain by Pen Press

All paper used in the printing of this book has been made from wood grown in managed, sustainable forests.

ISBN13: 978-1-78003-116-3

Printed and bound in the UK
Pen Press is an imprint of
Indepenpress Publishing Limited
25 Eastern Place
Brighton
BN2 1GJ

A catalogue record of this book is available from the British Library

Cover design by Jacqueline Abromeit

For my friends Winn Birkett and Lyn Downey,

who is also my cousin, who tell me

my writings are readable.

ONE

1985

Gillian moved slowly indoors, still reading the article. The reporter followed her, uninvited, into the pretty living room of the cottage. Gillian's golden retriever brought up the rear.

She came to the end of the article and looked up, unseeingly. Some of the colour had left her face.

'Well?' prompted her visitor, after a moment.

Gillian's eyes fell again to the Bowland Advertiser and News. 'Major Iain Hampshire,' she read out, a fine edge of scorn to her voice, 'is going to look into the affairs of Falcon Mill. Hopeful that…' Her hand shook as she ran her eye rapidly down the newsprint. 'Where were you five months ago, Major Playboy Hampshire? Stupidly lost in the South American jungle. Playing soldiers.' She threw the paper down on the saddle stool near the empty hearth.

'He's a bit of a hero, you know,' pointed out the author of the news item. 'Got himself and his men out when his helicopter was shot down by guerrillas. Got captured. Escaped. Lived off the land. Got caught again. Got valuable info…'

'Escaped again,' chanted Gillian, not letting herself feel even faintly impressed. She studied the report again.

There was a pause while the reporter decided how to word his next bombshell. Jasper nudged his mistress's hand with his nose. He was not used to strangers coming in with her in the middle of the day. This, he wanted to remind her, was the time of day she took him for a run. Gillian looked down into his affectionate brown eyes, routine far from her thoughts.

'You'll not know then,' came the careful voice behind her, 'that he moved in yesterday?'

She whirled round. 'Where?' Involuntarily she turned her eyes to the wall beside the fireplace as if they could pierce two feet of stone and see, in the middle distance, the seventeenth century manor house, dreaming there in the misty September sunshine – her family's home for two hundred years and hers for the last twenty-two. Until Easter this year.

'Well – Falcon Park.' Terry Dunlop sounded apologetic.

Resisting the impulse, which she knew to be unfair – he was, after all, only the bringer of news – to order him to get out, to throw something at the wall, she kicked aside the saddle stool in her path and began to prowl about. After a few minutes she sat down in an armchair with a sigh, indicating that he might as well take the other one. She had known Terry Dunlop all her life, had seen a lot of him in days gone by when she was usually doing something newsworthy enough for a mention in the weekly local newspaper, which Terrence Dunlop Senior owned.

Now she was sitting communing with herself Terry could study her face in detail, the beautiful face which had appeared so often in his paper over the years, laughing and animated. How fined down it had become! He had noticed already, when he was waiting at her door and she came cycling towards him along Church Row, that her long silvery hair had been cropped at her perfect jawline since last he saw her; that the narrow jeans she was wearing were much narrower than she could possibly have got into five months ago. That was when Hampshire Holdings foreclosed, when Gillian and her father left Falcon Park and went their separate ways.

For the rest, her eyes – jewel green – were still her most striking feature, their lashes thick, long and dark. Her complexion, attractively tinted by nature, was as flawless as ever. But there was a fundamental change to be felt in her and a fine-boned new strength. Now that she was over the first shock of the news he had brought her, there was an air of pensiveness about her that had certainly not been present in times past.

'What do you want me to say?' she asked at last in a flat voice.

He reluctantly broke off his survey and became brisk and professional. 'If you could just let me have your comments…'

'My comments would not be printable in a family newspaper. Nor would I like my mother to read them. My aunt sends her a copy of your paper every week.'

'Does she?' he exclaimed, diverted and gratified. 'Well, I suppose she likes to keep up with all the local goings-on, seeing she was in the thick of things till a year or so ago.'

'Three, actually. Can I keep this? I'll pay you for it of course.'

He waved a dismissing hand. 'If you'd just tell me what you think about it.'

'I don't know what I think. I'll have to, well, think.'

'Can I come back later when you've thunk?' he asked eagerly. A splendid idea came to him. 'Can I take you out to dinner tonight?'

An unkind retort sprang to her mind but was not voiced. This was followed by a novel thought: why not? When had she last been taken out to dinner? Should she let him though? If he meant the Grange, for instance, the cost…

'We could go to the Grange,' he declared. 'It's Friday but they might have a table. I'll ring up. If they haven't we'll go to Chipping or Lancaster or somewhere. When shall I pick you up?'

She was cornered and regretted that she had not said a firm no earlier. She would have to go through with it now, she supposed. She had got through all sorts of new experiences these last few months; one more would not harm her. Had any of them harmed her? She would have to have a think about that too. 'I don't finish work till half past seven,' she said.

'You should join a union!'

'And it takes about quarter of an hour to get home and half an hour to get ready.'

'Quarter past eight, then,' he said cheerfully, getting up from his chair and making for the door before she could change her mind.

His mini embarked upon a six-point turn in the narrow street. She watched it roar off unsuitably down the row between the cottages and the churchyard then turn left into the main road at the end.

'Thunk,' she said to Jasper, laughing a little now the tension had eased. 'I must remember that word!'

Jasper went across the road to inspect the church railings. His mistress had not moved from the doorway. She was making herself look across the fields and parkland towards her old home. She felt it ought to look different now that it contained an interloper. A wave of sickening frustration engulfed her. Whoever he was and whatever he was going to do, this Major Iain Hampshire – *it was too late.*

'Useless!' she hissed.

Jasper trotted enquiringly over to her, wagging his tail.

'Come on then. What are we waiting for? No – not that way.' Better to face some curious stares in the village. The Bowland Advertiser and News arrived at the newsagent-cum-post office at about eleven o'clock every Friday so the news would be out all around Great Bowland by now. The tom-toms would have been busy for the best part of two and a half hours. Smoke signals would have reached all corners of the valley and all the folds and crannies of Longbow Fell. It was a wonder news had not reached the farm before she had left it shortly after two o'clock. She was glad Terry Dunlop had come to tell her about it. Forewarned was indeed forearmed.

She began to run down the row in the wake of the mini. Jasper, bounding ahead, looked back at her saying, in body language, 'I should just think so!'

*****

Liz rushed out of the tackroom as Gillian pedalled over the worn cobbles of Gracemire's stableyard.

'Have you heard?' Liz bawled urgently.

'Yes,' called back Gillian, wheeling her bicycle into its usual place in one of the centuries old stone farm buildings which surrounded the yard on three sides. Liz, her cousin and employer, ran in after her, excited but anxious too. 'It's no good asking me what I think because I haven't thunk,' Gillian got in first.

'What do you think will happen? Will he give everything back to Uncle Giles?'

'Who? This Major Hamshank or whatever he calls himself? I doubt it. Why should he?'

'Well – reinstate him at the Mill, then?'

'I doubt that too. Did you know he's landed? He's at the Park.'

'No!'

'So I've been told. He got here yesterday sometime. He's probably hiding from the Press.'

'Wow – yes! They'll be on to him like starving wolves. What else do you know? Who told you?'

'Terry Dunlop did.'

Liz digested this in silence for a moment. 'And what did you tell him?'

'I've not told him anything yet. I might tonight, though, if I can think what. I'm going out to dinner with him.'

'With Terry Dunlop?' Liz squeaked.

'I can't think why I said I'd go. He's going to try and get in at the Grange.'

Liz began to laugh. 'And what is Fairy Godfather Munro going to say about that?'

Gillian had not thought of that. 'Perhaps they'll be booked up,' she said hopefully. Munro was the truest friend one could possibly have, but how would her French-African Dutch uncle view her arrival at the restaurant he now managed, at a time like this, with the local reporter?

*****

But Munro was expecting her: had even reserved a good table. It had not occurred to Gillian that Terry would use her name to get into the Grange on a popular night.

She eyed Munro uneasily as her chattering companion escorted her up the entrance steps. Terry fell silent when he caught sight of the tall, black impressive figure waiting for them on the threshold. How would he greet them, she wondered? With the trenchant Lancashire accent he could assume without warning? In potent silence?

But Munro's normal accent was as ever it had been during the two years he worked as general factotum at Falcon Park. He took her shawl from her with the correct degree of professional reverence and guided them to their table, drawing out her chair and settling her with graceful movements. Then he left them in the hands of a waiter.

That hurdle cleared, Gillian turned her attention to Terry. A spirited discussion was taking place with the waiter. What to have being settled, the waiter departed. A flow of words washed over her. She listened to him, rather touched by his obvious delight in being out with her. Soon she relaxed; he was really quite entertaining; she was enjoying herself. The food arrived and was excellent. How lovely to eat something not cooked by oneself!

Peaches filled with cheese paté had been disposed of and so had the homemade soup. Fillets of sole and various accompaniments were on the point of arrival and Terry had just leaned towards her, about to tell her something she sensed immediately was going to be about what was uppermost in her mind, when a sudden hush fell upon the room.

Her back was to the door but a large ornate mirror was on the wall above her companion's head. Reflected in it, Munro was bringing in a newcomer. The back of her neck began to prickle. Her breathing stopped. This, she knew without a shadow of doubt, could only be the interloper.

'Don't look now,' whispered Terry, 'but Major Hampshire's just landed.'

'Yes,' replied Gillian carefully. 'I can see him in that mirror.'

'Recognised him from the six o'clock news then did you?'

'No – I was still at work at six.' She was not going to ask about it.

She did not need to: Terry was going to tell her anyway and about the Major's longer and more personal appearance in the regional programme after the news. He leaned back as the next course was placed in front of him. Around the well-proportioned dining room the normal buzz and muted clatter was resuming following the hush that had fallen upon it when the man who was well and truly in the news arrived.

'God – he looks rough! He didn't look too bad on the box in colour.'

Gillian transferred a modest pile of French fries from a serving dish and helped herself to asparagus, onion rings and petits pois. While Terry was piling large helpings onto his oval plate her eyes were drawn irresistibly back to the mirror.

The long curtains were not yet drawn and the velvet night framed the two men in the corner. Munro was murmuring something which was briefly acknowledged, his handsome face and superb physique in startling contrast to the harsh weathered features and emaciated frame of the seated figure.

And yet, Gillian noticed reluctantly, the Major was not diminished as most other men would have been, fit or otherwise. The image that had been building up in her imagination all afternoon slipped away into oblivion – an image of a swashbuckling, conceited, selfish jet-setter who played at being a soldier like royalty when he should be attending his father's deathbed, taking his family firm's reins and, above all, preventing premature foreclosures at other people's family mills.

Terry wolfed down a few mouthfuls, eager to continue his tale. 'They finally managed to get through to some embassy outpost or other somewhere unpronounceable – it took them a bit to convince the officials of their recent encounters – then they got flown off to Washington for debriefing. That was last week sometime. They had to wait then till one of our Defence lot flew over there to complete the debriefing process. That's why the news didn't break till now. Had to make sure it was all on the level. The Americans are very pleased with the information.'

'Which was what?'

'Too hush-hush to talk about in detail. Mainly about guerrilla activities and a big drug processing set-up no one knew about in the middle of the jungle. Our lot's just glad to have five of its best men back again. The other two got killed, though.'

With great precision Gillian dissected an onion ring and tidily loaded it onto her fork, her thoughts with the families and loved-ones of those who had died. A wave of shame overcame her. Her preconceived notions had been unfair probably. She was determined not to feel any compassion for the new head of Hampshire Holdings, however. She stole another look at him before dealing with an asparagus tip. Yes, he did look rough. What a wreck he must have looked, they must all have looked, when they first reached civilization after all those months, their clothes in tatters, unshaven, their hair unbarbered.

Her artist's eye could now see that beneath the ravaged surface of his face the over-prominent bones were good: the cheekbones high and well spaced, his brow broad and well-proportioned, his jaw the jaw of an aggressor. For all his haggardness his mouth was definitely handsome, she allowed, his lips curly and neither thick nor too thin with an attractive indentation somewhere beneath the lower one. His eyes were grey, narrowed and bleak.

And, through the mirror, they were looking directly into hers.

Startled, her own eyes widened, her lips parted and a rosy blush tinted her tanned face. For a timeless moment the world receded.

Then the reflected image of Munro's shapely back intervened and the spell broke. The sweet trolley arriving brought her back to the present. Terry was asking her what she fancied.

'Whatever you're having.'

When the trolley was wheeled away leaving two loaded dishes Terry made up his mind. 'Gill…I mean Miss Falconer…'

'Oh call me Gillian. I'm not the daughter of the manor now. I'm just a cook-stroke-groom.' She stopped suddenly. Had she said that too loudly and too fast? Had her voice carried as far as that corner table? The Major's hearing would no doubt be highly acute if he'd been creeping about the jungle in danger all that time.

'Gillian – you were mentioned.'

'*I* was?' She was appalled.

'The interviewer, it was a woman of course, was rabbiting on at him about his broken romance and getting nowhere. Then she asked him if the knowledge that the former owner of Falcon Mill had two pretty daughters had influenced his decision to come up north?'

It took several seconds for Gillian to assimilate the enormity of this. 'That's totally intolerable,' she hissed.

'He seemed to think so too.'

'What did he say?'

Nothing. He just looked. Then he said he hadn't as yet learned the name of the former owner but would probably be meeting him sooner or later if he was still living in the area.'

Gillian began to force down the meringue concoction Terry had chosen. It might as well have been cold porridge. She gave up the struggle after a few mouthfuls.

'Shall we dance?' Terry asked when his dish was scraped clean.

'No. I mean…'

He stood up looking down at her, pleased that he had shaken her cool poise without arousing her enmity. 'Come on – you show 'em who's boss.'

'Whatever do you mean?' she asked faintly. But she allowed him to take her hand and lead her away towards the sounds of disco dancing.

As they danced (and she danced very well indeed, as did her partner) her eyes at first kept straying towards the arched doorway. Then, realising this, she took herself firmly in hand and refused to allow them to stray in that direction again until the early hours of the morning when the disc jockey, after several encores of the last waltz, finally switched off his systems.

Tired but very happy Terry put her tenderly into his little car and drove her home. He was wondering if his cup was about to be filled to overflowing and she was going to let him kiss her, when something occurred to her.

'Terry?'

'Mmm?'

'Are you... Am I... Is my name going to appear in next week's Advertiser?'

'No.'

'But you won't be able to charge tonight's dinner to expenses if you don't write something about me. You did say you were going to come back later to see what I'd thunk.'

'I've no intention of charging tonight's dinner to expenses. As far as I'm concerned it was a night to remember. Unless you want me to put any comments in?'

'It was certainly a night to remember. No – of course I don't. The last thing I want is publicity. But I have had time to think now – while we were dancing, actually, seeing the music was too loud to talk.'

'And?'

'If you should feel like printing my comments I wouldn't mind you putting it on record that Gillian Falconer welcomes the arrival of Major et cetera in the valley and hopes that his investigations and ultimate decisions will help the dire unemployment problem in this district.'

'What does Miss Gillian Falconer think about him invading her old home?'

'Gillian Falconer is glad the old place is being lived in again and hopes he soon finds a suitable buyer as presumably he will not be staying in Great Bowland forever. It costs a bomb to run. Don't put that! Why are you not writing all this down?'

'Because it's pitch dark in here. It's all gone down into memory though. I might use it if you're sure. If you change your mind ring me at the office before Tuesday and I'll scrub it. I'll talk to some other locals and get their comments as well and put them around yours. I'll talk to himself too. If television crews can, I can.'

It was indeed pitch dark. He did not see the glint of battle in her eye as they got out of the car. He hovered hopefully at her door under the towering friendly shadow of the church opposite. The moon slid out of the clouds and back in again. Indoors Jasper whined in anticipation.

I'm not getting invited in I suppose?' Life could not be that good. Life was not that good. He was, however, allowed to gratify a sudden inclination on Gillian's part to be kissed. Just kissed. Five months was a long time to go unkissed at twenty-two. Not that she wanted to be kissed by anyone, in particular for his own sake. But Terry had given her a very interesting evening. He smelt nice too. So she put her arms round his neck and let him kiss her again: several times.

'That was a very interesting evening,' she said. 'Thank you.'

'And goodnight, I suppose,' he sighed, without rancour. 'Oh well.'

TWO

For the duration of breakfast at the farm the next day Gillian was very aware that the morning newspapers were piled upon the dresser; that there were more of them than usual; that they were all folded so that certain articles of news were uppermost.

After that she managed to restrain her curiosity just long enough to clear away that meal and make a few preparations for the next. But now, alone in the kitchen, apart from the two cats, she allowed herself to sit down at the long refectory table and reach out for the tempting pile.

She bent her head over a blotched photograph in one of the papers, taken before the five men in the headlines left by plane for Washington, trying to guess which bush of hair Major Iain Hampshire might be lurking beneath. The very recent army haircut she had seen last night obviously came later, either before or after the shaving. Idly she wondered which. Not that she was remotely interested she told herself, pulling the Guardian out of the pile to see what they had misprinted.

The fingers of the clock on the high shelf over the range moved on. The clock cleared its throat. It chimed. Gillian read on quickly, tossing the papers aside as she finished each article.

They informed her about some of the more hair-raising adventures the seven men had got into with rebel guerrillas and how two of them lost their lives; about the near starvation they endured living off the land during their covert progress in what they hoped was the right direction without maps and with only their memories, one damaged compass and an occasional glimpse of the stars to guide them; about the vast and hidden narcotic operation they accidentally located when they were at their lowest ebb, especially their leader who was in a fever following a deadly insect bite; about their treatment at the hands of the guards who captured them; their subsequent escape. And, finally, about the moment they struggled out of the jungle into the open sunlight and saw before them with unbelievable relief the river they had been hearing for the last hour or so of their slow and painful search for civilization.

None of the men could yet, it appeared, stop over-reacting to any unexpected noise or movement; could not stand people standing or moving about behind them. It would take time, said the Times, for these men to recover from the physical and mental injuries inflicted upon them.

'It was their own faults for volunteering to go in the first place,' Gillian told Ozymandias, when at last she had finished reading. 'They knew it would be very dangerous.' But the censure in her voice sounded hollow. Ozymandias grinned enigmatically back at her from a rocking chair by the range.

*****

The clock cleared its throat again. This time Gillian heard it. She leapt to her feet. For the next twenty minutes she rushed about the kitchen, the newspapers scattered and abandoned on the table. Efficiently, but with less than her usual finesse, she hurled ingredients into bowls, hacked up onions, walloped pastry about, adjusted the heat of various rings and plates on the modern hob, peered into the ongoing broth pan and attended to various other details. Finally she wrenched open the door of the oven in the old range and heaved in the enormous hotpot she had thrown together. She closed the door upon it and took a deep breath.

On cue the men began to troop in for their mid-morning usuals. At breakfast, which Gillian had cooked as normal, the men had tactfully played her game of pretending nothing out of the ordinary had happened. They knew all about the new tenant up at the Park of course, but had kept off this highly sensitive subject, talking instead about the final cricket match of the season due to take place that afternoon. This subject was still under discussion. In fact an argument had developed in which Austin the shepherd was taking no part, as to whether they would be playing their first reserve, i.e. Austin, or whether Munro, who had been forced to miss one or two matches recently due to his new job at the Grange, would be able to take his usual place in the team.

Austin was quite untroubled by these speculations. If they wanted him they could come and get him from the pub, which was where he'd be, seeing that he lived there. He rarely bothered to attend his team's home matches unless he was called upon to play. Today's special gala tea in the pavilion afterwards might be worth looking in on though, especially if Gillian was going to be there, which she probably would be, as Liz was on the Wives' Committee and Liz roped Gillian in for most things now she had her working for her. In the meantime, why was Brian stood gangling there, his head in the rafters, blocking his view of Gillian?

Casually, Austin lifted one long leg and aimed a kick at his brother, who jumped and spluttered into his pint mug of hot milk and sugar.

*****

By the time the mid-morning ride was heard returning to the stables the last of the bread and butter and Gillian's homemade fruitcake had vanished. Liz must have ridden in ahead of the others because she collided with her husband, Reg, on the doorstep in her rush to get to Gillian.

'Whoops!' she squeaked, clutching him for a moment to steady herself. Then she darted between Austin and Old Jem, pushed Brian, who bent like a willow, out of her path and broke into a run to get round the unpushable bulk of Sam the blacksmith.

She flung herself into one of the rocking chairs by the fire as the last of the men left the kitchen.

'What did he look like?' she asked breathlessly as if their very brief discussion earlier had not been interrupted.

'Who – Munro?'

'I *know* what Munro looks like, idiot! Gorgious. No – *him*. Was he covered with scars?'

'I couldn't see any actual scars. He was four tables away and I could only see his reflection. Those blotches on his face could have been grazes I suppose.'

'Didn't you look at him properly in the flesh when you went off to dance?'

'I have not so far seen him in the flesh. I didn't look. Do you want your coffee now?'

'I bet Munro told him who you were, though. I'll get coffee. You get on with your slaughtering. Gillian was cutting up a blood-coloured beetroot. 'It's beetroot. It must be hotpot. It must be Saturday. Did he let one of his slaves serve him or did he wait upon him himself?'

'He got the full VIP treatment.'

'Are you bitter?'

Gillian's knife paused. 'Should I be?'

'Who are you asking – you or me?'

'I don't know. Since Terry first told me about it yesterday I've been…'

'In mental disarray?' suggested Liz after waiting a few moments for Gillian to choose the right words.

'Sort of. I don't think I'm bitter against him himself. Well – I am, but it's not logical to blame him for not being in the right place at the right time. Perhaps I'll get over it. It all depends on what happens next. About the mill I mean.'

'And what attitude, asked Liz, greatly daring, 'is the previous owner's pretty daughter going to adopt towards the man himself?'

The knife resumed its attack with new viciousness. So Liz too had heard about that hackle-raising question on television. Had everyone? 'I can only speak for the lesser of the two,' she produced at last, 'who is going to give the new broom the widest of all wide berths.'

Liz eyed her cousin mischievously. The kettle at her elbow switched itself off. 'Since when,' she asked, pouring boiling water into flowered beakers, 'did Laura ever give any male, over or under the age of consent, a wide berth?' Her glance went beyond Gillian to the doorway. A smile of pure delight swept over her small face. 'Come *in,*' she exclaimed.

The red stained knife still in her hand Gillian whipped round to face the door as, light as a cat, the Major stepped into the kitchen. Something instantly suppressed flashed across his face.

Slowly he transferred his gaze from the knife to the fierce green eyes of the girl holding it. He was still yards from her but for a split second it had been as if he had flung himself at her, his whipcord body bearing hers backwards, his steel grip disarming her knife hand.

Liz opened her mouth then closed it again. Her periwinkle eyes widened. She shivered suddenly with excitement at whatever it was that had just entered the room with this man.

Gillian laid down her knife with studied care. 'Good morning,' she said.

'Good morning, Miss Falconer. My name's Hampshire. Iain Hampshire.'

So Munro had told him who she was last night. Well of course he had. Obviously.

'We thought it might be,' nodded Liz.

'I'm looking for a lady called Liz.'

Liz walked across the kitchen to stand in front of him. She had to look a long way up to meet his eyes.

'When you've found her,' she said, 'how should she address you?'

'I hope that she, and everyone else, will call me Iain.'

'Well Iain, now you've found me what can I do for you?'

'I'd like to ride if there's a horse to spare.'

They all listened for a moment to the sounds of horses and ponies departing.

'They've gone without you, Liz,' remarked Gillian, going off to put a pan on with an air of one who has work to do and no time for social chit-chat.

'Austin's having his weekly treat,' dismissed Liz.

'Austin's your husband?'

'No – he's our shepherd. We're booked up till three-thirty, at least the heavyweights are. There's a Shetland free but…'

Trust Liz, smouldered Gillian. She, Gillian, was taking out the three-thirty ride. She'd be inviting him to lunch next!

'You can have Barney at three-thirty, though.'

'Why not Bridgenorth?' enquired Gillian tartly over her shoulder, 'seeing he…'

'You're riding Bridgenorth,' cut in Liz. She turned back to the Major. 'What about lunch? Have you had it yet? There's plenty extra if you want to stay. Gillian always makes a huge hotpot on Saturdays and some of the men go home so there's always some left. We often have it fried up for breakfast on Sundays.'

'It sounds irresistible.'

'It is. It is. She puts all the week's leftovers in it. That's settled then. There's my husband look!' She pointed through the window. 'I'll get him and he can show you around: boundaries and so forth. You'll want to know how far your empire reaches.' She ran off leaving the other two alone in the kitchen.

She should invite him to sit down, Gillian supposed. The caring half of her nature wanted to. He looked leaner still this morning in the navy blue sweater he was wearing – thinner even than Brian. But Brian was only seventeen and had not yet the great breadth of shoulder that this man had. And Brian, six feet five inches tall and still growing, walked with an apologetic stoop. There was nothing remotely apologetic or stooping about the man who had now gone to lean those wide shoulders against the wall.

'Miss Falconer…'

Gillian continued rinsing pint mugs and did not look at him. 'Yes, Major Hampshire?'

'What were you going to say about that horse?'

'Bridgenorth? Only that he belongs to you.'

'What makes you say that?'

'He was my father's. So that makes him yours now.' She did not add the words *like everything else* but they hung in the air. With a steady hand Gillian ladled sugar into a jug.

'Does anyone at Hampshire Holdings know we own a horse?'

'Probably not.'

'Who pays for his keep?'

Gillian took her time levering off the lid of the custard tin before replying with a shrug: 'He earns his keep.'

'I wish some other past and present members of the group could say the same for themselves.'

Slowly she turned to look at him. What was behind those words?

But Liz had flitted back in, towing Reg. Iain Hampshire removed his shoulders from the wall and Liz lost no time in putting him and Reg on first name terms. Then she shooed them out of the kitchen.

Gillian braced herself for a string of exclamations. Nothing happened immediately, however. She glanced at Liz and saw with astonishment that tears were rolling down her face.

'Whatever's the matter?'

'Oh Gillian,' wailed Liz.' Did you not see his hands?'

'No – I didn't look at him much.'

Liz got a tissue out of the pocket of her jodhpurs and wiped her face and blew her nose. 'I wondered why he didn't offer to shake hands,' she managed in a stifled voice. 'He just…just…'

'Yes – I saw. He didn't quite salute. His heels didn't quite click.' Gillian was not going to admit that she found his way of acknowledging introductions, of avoiding handshakes, rather… What? Intriguing? All right – *attractive.* The stylish movement made you forget for a moment the dreadful condition he was in.

And dreadful his state was, viewed at close quarters during the few brief times she had made herself look at him. Odd that she hadn't spotted his hands. She felt no revulsion, of course, and yet she felt no pity either as Liz obviously did. Very strange. What she would not mind doing, if he was going to insist on foisting himself into their midst for any length of time, was try and fatten him up a bit – like Brian. She had been trying to fatten up Brian since she started working here at Gracemire Farm.

She reviewed the meal she was preparing. Would the stewed apples be too acid for his deprived digestion? On Saturdays, as well as stewed apples, they had for afters any leftover cake chopped up and smothered in hot custard. There was quite a lot of it today. Would he fancy this homely offering if apples were too acid?

Her musings at this stage were interrupted by Liz, swearing. Mog had spent the morning asleep on the top of the dresser in the shallow space under the beams. He had roused himself, had a good stretch, then used Liz's shoulder as a convenient staging post on his descent to ground level.

'Anyway,' said Liz fiercely, as Mog stalked away, 'I think he's gorgious.'

'Like Munro?'

'Yes.'

'What do you mean – yes…? Munro's a great, bounding, healthy, very handsome man. How can you possibly compare him with that great lanky, hawkfaced, battered…?'

'You wait,' called Liz, heading for the door, her sunny spirits restored. 'You wait.'

'No I won't,' Gillian told the kitchen. 'Why should I?'

*****

As Liz had said, some of the men went home for lunch on Saturdays so there was just the one sitting. Shortly after twelve o'clock seven people gathered round the scrubbed table. Reg took the carver at the head of the long table. Those who usually sat on his left all moved down a place to make room for the guest.

Liz helped herself and everyone else who wanted it to broth, talking all the time. She was telling Iain about the cricket match and recommending tea in the pavilion.

'Tea'll be from about half past four so you'll be back from your ride. Everyone in the village will be there so it'll be a good opportunity to meet the locals.'

'If the Press isn't there to mob him first,' remarked Christine, Liz's assistant.

As the meal continued, Liz's ideas about dealing with the Press became more and more fanciful, 'And Jem could fetch the bull along,' she concluded as the last coffee cup was emptied.

'Ar,' agreed Old Jem.

There was nothing wrong with the hero's appetite Gillian reflected drily as she loaded the dishwasher. He had had broth, two sizeable helpings of hotpot (but no trimmings) and two large dishfuls of cake and custard. He and Reg were now taking their ease in the rocking chairs, a cat on each lap, cigar smoke twirling about their heads. Very cosy. Well, she was off home now. She needed a respite before facing that damned ride. What sort of a rider was he anyway? For all they knew he might never have ridden before; might just have booked a ride to worm his way into local life. If he fell off, *she* wasn't going to try and pick him up. That was for sure.

There was no need to bid anyone any ceremonious farewells, she decided, as she left the kitchen. She would just melt away quietly. She edged her way through the press of horses and riders preparing for off in the stable yard, pausing to tighten Munchman's girth a notch and give his rider a leg up.

Wheeling her bicycle, she made her way around the edge of the yard, past stable doorways, past the tackroom and the feed store, past the wide open door of the forge, its fire low, falling into its weekend sleep. Picking her way over the cobbles she did not notice a tall figure standing by the stone archway leading out into the road until she almost walked into him. He must have crept out after her and stalked her into the yard, she thought, and taken up his position here to ambush her. He was continuing to wage jungle warfare in

Great Bowland! Annoyed, she now discovered that he had somehow removed her bicycle from her clutches.

'I'll drive you home,' he said. 'I want to talk to you. This will fit in the back.'

For a dreadful moment she wondered what he had driven himself here in. If the Rolls was out there parked on the verge she would just turn round and walk back the way she had come and keep walking.

Bile rising in her, she followed her property through the archway. And there in the grassy area between the high wall and the road was the strangest vehicle she had ever seen. An involuntary smile appeared on her face. Anything less like a Rolls Royce she had yet to see. She had never seen anything like it before, even on films. It must have been one of Her Majesty's Army's more secret weapons. It was low, painted in camouflage colours and lethal looking.

'Do they know you've borrowed it?' she enquired.

'They turned a blind eye. I was in a hurry to get away.' He unlocked the rear door and put in her bicycle with minimum fuss. He opened the front passenger door with a bow in keeping with a deluxe limousine. She curled up neatly and put herself in. She was still studying the business-like safety straps when he got in beside her. His nearness was strictly correct as those terrible hands adjusted her harness and fastened her in securely. Then they were off, the acceleration making her gasp.

'You will have to direct me.'

'Left here then on to the church. I live by it.'

'Very beautiful country.'

Very conventional, thought Gillian. We'll be discussing the weather next. The jeep was travelling slowly now for some reason.

'Especially now autumn's here. It's early this year. The heather's been out ages.'

'And not a dark satanic mill in sight.'

'There's one over there. It belongs to you.'

He glanced over the shining sweep of green and gold countryside on his right. A large grey stone building, like a natural outcrop, nestled half a mile away, its vast wheel visible.

'How long since the wheel worked?'

'Right up until after the war,' she replied, a note of pride in her voice.

'Your friends have a lovely place,' he offered next.

'Gracemire? Yes – it's very old, some of it – sixteenth century. It was a hunting lodge.'

This brought them to the turning by the ancient sunken church. 'My cottage is at the far end. You'd better not drive up – you'll never turn around.'

'Like to bet?'

Apparently he was coming in. Jasper's ecstatic greetings were cut short while he subjected his mistress's new companion to a thorough investigation. Sniffing loudly he circled them.

'Will I do?' he asked the dog.

'Won't you sit down?' asked Gillian, politely, indicating a chintz armchair. 'I'll just give him some milk.' Jasper bounded after her into the kitchen.

Gillian opened the fridge and poured milk for the dog. This operation could not have taken longer than one minute but when she returned, somewhat uncertainly, to the living room, she stopped in her tracks. There was no need to brace herself for whatever it was he wanted to talk to her about. Her visitor was fast asleep.

Surely he must be feigning! One could not fall asleep so suddenly. But there was something convincing about his drooped head, his slack hands. At a loss Gillian wondered what to do. It could not be right to fall asleep so suddenly. Or had he passed out? Ought she to get help? She remembered that he was on the sick list. Was it blackouts he was suffering from? She thought of the army vehicle parked outside. No – he would hardly be driving about in that and wanting to ride horses if he was subject to blackouts.

Jasper trotted in and bustled over. Her hand on his collar stopped him as he was about to lick that limp scarred hand, its curled fingers with their broken nails partly concealing a black-rimed palm.

In fact, she decided, he looked perfectly all right – better than he did last night at the Grange: less worn. His breathing was light and regular. More or less satisfied that he was not in a coma she turned away. She would like to go on inspecting his features and trying to decide what he would look like when he was fit again, but scruples would not allow her to take any further advantage of his unconsciousness. She moved over to the sofa. She would put her feet up for half an hour or so. Three o'clock would be early enough to waken him. She settled herself among the cushions and Jasper curled himself into a circle mid-way between the sleeper and the sofa, his black nose nestling in his tail.

Peace descended on the cool room with its pretty sprigged wallpaper and chintzes, its glints of planished copper, its autumn carpet and polished dark boards.

Shortly before three o'clock Gillian went silently upstairs to change into riding clothes. There was no need for a jacket or sweater in today's unusual warmth. She eyed her show-jumping jodhpurs, skin tight, wickedly expensive and almost new.

No – she would stick to her workaday ones, well-worn but standing up to it as so they ought – they were expensive too: all her clothes were because they all dated back to the days before the crash. Those she wore nowadays had had to be taken in. She chose an understated parchment blouse, its simplicity ornamented by a scant scattering of innocent little acorn motifs.

She regarded her reflection for a moment or two. As usual she was wearing no makeup at all and it was doubtful if any artifice could have improved upon the beauty nature had bestowed upon the delicately chiselled contours of her face.

It was time to make some coffee and wake up the sleeper. She could put it off no longer. Jasper's brown eyes watched brightly from their nest of golden plumes as she put her visitor's coffee cup down on the copper log box by his chair. She stepped back and coughed to rouse him.

His rousing was instantaneous. He leapt forward and seized her throat in a death-grip.

In the terrifying moment before her senses left her Jasper leapt too. In the pandemonium the two snarling faces merged in the red mist before her eyes as the dog's fangs sank into her assailant's arm.

It took a moment for her to realize that she was not going to die, that the grip that was taking her life had slackened. A pair of horrified grey eyes was hovering inches before her blurred vision. The dog was growling still, trying with all his considerable strength to drag him off by his sleeve. But the current was switched off.

'Oh my God!' he groaned. His head sank slowly onto her shoulder and stayed there, moving slightly as the dog jerked at his arm.

'Stop it, Jasper,' she croaked. 'Sit.'

The dog stared at her in astonishment, letting go of the sleeve. He knew it was her voice but it had never sounded like that before.

She would have to take charge. His arms were around her now, his weight nearly causing her weakened legs to give way. She could feel him drawing comfort from her. He would probably regret it later, regard it as a display of weakness. She must say something prosaic – if she could speak intelligibly with her mangled throat.

'Your...coffee's...going cold,' she articulated tinnily.

He raised his head and moved back from her, his eyes on her throat. Through her considerable pain and distress she suddenly hoped desperately that he would not start apologising, would not become abject. Then she felt rather than saw him snap back into full control. Her eyes were watering but not so much so that she missed seeing him once again make that slight movement which conveyed a salute, the clicking of military heels, a bow.

'Ma'am – I apologise.'

She would not let herself finger her damaged throat, 'Did I interrupt a bad dream or something?'

'Or something. Please don't do it again. I might not be so lucky next time.'

'*You* might not?'

'Or you. Sit down for goodness sake before you fall down. I don't want to have to catch you or indeed touch you at all with these hands.'

'You already have,' she managed faintly. 'Did it hurt you too?'

'Not at all. Not physically. They're unsightly but not painful any more. Where's your coffee?'

She seated herself carefully in the opposite chair as he marched into the kitchen. An hysterical chuckle tried to rear itself past her painful vocal chords. *Abject?*

'We have to plan.'

She took a cautious sip from the cup he handed to her. 'Some other time. I've got to get back.'

'You'd better stop here. I'll take your place, supervise things, catch people when they fall off, whatever it is you do. Someone else can navigate no doubt. I don't want anyone to see those marks. I don't know which I relish least: them being taken for what they are or mistaken for love bites.'

This was too fast for her. She put down her cup. 'I'm going. People can think what they like.'

'Have you a scarf?'

She dragged herself out of the room and toiled upstairs. It took some time to arrange a wisp of chiffon the same green as her eyes. The flimsy texture rubbed her tender bruises.

Iain was in the kitchen when she came downstairs. He was rolling down his sleeve and had evidently found plasters. So Jasper had drawn blood.

'Not bad,' he said, examining her handiwork. 'There's a bit showing there.' He pointed without touching her.

But Gillian was past caring. She was driven swiftly and safely to the stables. He had held the door open for her to get in. He had not attempted to help her with the safety harness. Physical contact between them was studiously avoided

THREE

As the athletics required to mount an eighteen-hand horse unaided (normally no trouble) were beyond her, Gillian moved Bridgenorth to the mounting block to get herself into the saddle. She was adjusting the stirrups when Liz appeared at her knee – unexpectedly because she ought to have been milking, it being Saturday: especially this Saturday when some of the men were playing cricket.

Gillian watched her cousin's expressive face as a series of emotions flitted across it like a film reel. First there was curiosity. Why had Gillian used the mounting block? Then the scarf was noted, twinkled at and judged to be an effort on Gillian's part to decorate herself, which could only be in Iain's honour. Then the sharp eyes spotted the marks under the shadow of her chin and widened disbelievingly. Next, amused speculation was chased off her face by acute suspicion. Finally Liz scanned Gillian's washed-out face.

'What happened?'

'I can't tell you now. I've got to go. Why aren't you milking?'

'Your voice! Your neck… What on earth did he do to you?' Her voice was rising and Sam, the blacksmith, strode out of the forge to see what was the matter.

'Hush, will you,' rasped Gillian.

Liz lowered her voice. 'Tell me what happened. If that swine has hurt you I'll get him flung out! Sam will chuck him out. Sam'll *kill* him!'

Sam spoke in his rumbling deep voice. 'What did he do?'

She would have to tell them quickly. Already some of the riders across the yard were casting interested looks in their direction.

'He took me home and came in. He said he wanted to talk to me but he fell asleep as soon as he sat down, for some reason. So I let him sleep for a bit. When I had to waken him he must have thought he was back in the jungle and I was about to attack him.' She stopped, her voice nearly giving out.

'And…?'

'He leapt at me. Anyway, Jasper flew at him and he came to his senses immediately. He told me to put a scarf on. He apologised.' She could see, looking down into Liz's troubled face and Sam's forbidding one that, while they were both conceding that there might be mitigating circumstances, the Major had earned himself a large black question mark.

They all turned as Barney clopped up to them. From his back, Iain read the scene at a glance. He looked unsmilingly down at Liz, gave Gillian one penetrating glance then turned to regard the bearded Colossus, who looked steadily back at him conveying a wordless warning. Without appearing to be in any way intimidated, the Major wordlessly acknowledged the warning: seemed even to approve of it.

Liz let out a deep breath. 'Well – that's probably all right-ish then, or will be when your throat's better. I'm not needed for milking. Father Elphinstone's turned up thinking we'd be pushed. Austin too for some reason. So I'll have a lift as far as the cricket. Do my bit re the teas.'

Her foot disappeared into Sam's vast fist. With one economical movement the muscle-bound Vulcan put her up behind Gillian, his bulging biceps enough, in Liz's view, to frighten off a whole platoon of stranglers.

'Lead on, Claire!' Liz shouted across the yard. 'We'll catch you up. Go around behind the cricket field and head for the Trough.'

The other riders filed out after the dedicated fourteen-year-old.

'You can be rearguard,' Liz told Iain. 'We're doing a detour.' They watched him ride out of the yard before giving Bridgenorth the office to follow. 'He looks like a Cossack from the back,' approved Liz, already looking for reasons for forgiving him and restoring him to favour in Gillian's eyes – not that Gillian had so far shown any signs of being found favour with.

Gillian did not reply, saving her voice. Liz continued to discuss the matter with Gillian's back. 'We'll just have to wait and see,' she was saying. 'He's blotted his copy book, of course he has, and if he does anything like that again, even in his special circs., someone will have to do something. But perhaps he'll soon get used to not being in danger. And I daresay he was appalled when he realized what he'd done. And he's had a dreadful time, poor lad, and he must be feeling pretty miserable as well, going through all that then coming home to find he's been jilted and his father dead and the business all to pot. Not,' she added, the thought striking her, 'that he's the only one whose life's been turned upside-down and who's been jilted. You've quite a lot in common, really.' She began to giggle. 'You've not managed to give him a very wide berth so far, have you?'

'Will you stop shouting in my ear. There's Munro, look.'

'Where?' shouted Liz, diverted at once. 'I see him. Gillian – he's not got his shirt on!'

They were now nearing the pavilion. Liz was misquoting Hamlet, her cheek resting on Gillian's shoulder. Gillian was not listening. Nor was she looking at Munro, approaching them in immaculate white trousers, a gold cross on his broad black chest catching the sun. Another figure had Gillian's attention – a large, very English gentleman in his early fifties, lounging in a deckchair. He too was dressed in cricket whites but was, more conventionally, wearing a shirt – a beautifully laundered shirt, Gillian noted. Trust Laura!

'"How like an angel,"' finished Liz on an ecstatic sigh.

'Hello, Dad,' said Gillian.

Her father got easily to his feet and strolled across to them. 'Hello, Darling. How are you?'

'I'm all right.'

'You don't sound it. Got a sore throat?'

'A bit.'

'Taking anything for it?' His eyes were on Bridgenorth who was whickering at him and evincing great pleasure at seeing him again.

Liz put her hand on her uncle's shoulder. He paused in his inspection of the horse that was no longer his and lifted her down from her perch behind Gillian on the capacious saddle. Bridgenorth was in excellent condition. Satisfied, he looked up at his daughter again, not noticing her bruises.

'I want to see you later, Gillian,' he said. 'I've got something to tell you.' Someone called his name. 'I'd better be off.' He picked up his bat and saluted them with it. He already had his pads on. They watched his leisurely progress across the pitch as he went to take the vicar's place at the crease.

'I'd better be off too,' said Gillian, remembering her duties. The other riders could be seen about half a mile away, strung across the bright hillside.

'What happened to your neck?' asked Munro, a restraining hand on the bridle.

'You tell him, Liz.'

He stepped back, a steely tilt to his jaw.

'It's just been one damn thing after another since lunchtime yesterday,' she muttered to the horse as she turned and urged him into a trot.

She caught up with the others quite easily by taking a shorter route and letting Bridgenorth have his head. They made an heroic picture, thundering across Reg's pastures, flying over low walls, hedges and ditches known well to both horse and rider. The exercise quite revived her. Her throat was much easier now. She could nearly forget it for minutes at a time. The others watched as she trotted up to them across the sheep-cropped turf, admiration in most expressions. But what was passing through the mind of the rearguard it was impossible to fathom. After one quick look Gillian ignored him for the rest of the ride.

Several children jockeyed for position near her. They considered Gillian very good value. She listened to them with gratifying interest and their main aim was to make her laugh. They liked her laugh – it was genuine.

The rest of the ride was uneventful, even idyllic. Late September was producing a bonus of perfect days, misty with a hint of frost after dawn, turning slowly into molten gold, smiling and mellow through the long lazy afternoons.

The children did not manage to make Gillian laugh today but she listened to all the jokes they had saved up to tell her and smiled her lovely smile at them.

Back at the stables, she and Christine were dealing with the changeover to the next ride when the muted roar of the army jeep departing in the direction of Falcon Park was heard above the clatter. A strange bereft feeling came over Gillian. Annoyed with herself, she declined the offer of a lift behind Christine on Barney, choosing to walk back to the cricket field alone with her thoughts, hoping to restore some kind of order in her brain on the way.

*****

The first person Gillian saw when she arrived back at the cricket field was her immaculate sister, lying elegantly on an up-market recliner brought, no doubt, with its twin beside it in the Porsche parked nearby. The other recliner supported the limbs of an equally elegant male counterpart. Laura's looks always ensured that she was never without a creditable escort. Men liked to be seen with her as she was a fiery beauty with a mane of black curls, matt cream skin and a tall goddess body. Laura's other car, a Peugeot family saloon, was parked alongside the Porsche which meant that their father had come in it, presumably because he had different plans for after the match.

'Hallo Laura,' said Gillian, feeling as usual like a very young younger sister.

She did not look like one, however, and there was a flash of annoyance in Laura's Siamese cat eyes at her companion's reaction to her crisp introduction: 'This is Lance Drysdale, Gillian. Lance – my sister.'

'I say!' said Lance, standing up, drinking her in. 'Pleased to meet you.' He took her hand. '*Very* pleased to meet you. You…er. You're not a bit alike, are you? Haven't I seen you before somewhere?'

'We're half-sisters,' said Laura tersely.

'Yes… Well.' He seemed to be lost for words. Gillian extracted her hand. She knew perfectly well that he was unlikely to be as lost for words as he chose to appear. She knew who he was having attended a few country house sales with her mother in the olden days (which was probably where he had seen her before). Lance Drysdale was an auctioneer – a very good one too. Whoever heard of an auctioneer being lost for words?

'Dad's out, I see,' Gillian remarked. 'How many did he get?'

'Twenty six,' said Laura. She added with typical accuracy: 'He hit three sixes and a four so he didn't have to run much. What's the matter with your neck? Or shouldn't I ask?'

'Oh good,' said Gillian, ignoring this last. 'It's a bit hot for running.'

They watched Reg swipe a ball just short of the boundary. He made three runs but unfortunately his partner was run out. Munro would be in next, Gillian knew. 'I'm going to find Liz,' she said. 'See you later, perhaps.'

'Ra-ther!' enthused Lance, watching her until she disappeared round the pavilion.

Munro was there, waiting to go out, cricket pads strapped to his long legs. But there was no sign of Liz. Gillian sidled cautiously into the pavilion keeping out of Munro's range. She could see Liz, chattering as usual, at the other end of the building where she and three other wives were putting finishing touches to the gala tea.

Liz greeted her warmly and said: 'We're just pooling what we know about the new Lord of the Manor.'

The others exchanged startled glances. After all, Gillian was the deposed daughter of the manor. She showed no signs of minding, however, as she joined them and picked up a knife. One of the wives was cutting up three quiches the size of small cartwheels, provided by Gracemire's kitchen and brought by Reg earlier in the Land Rover.

Liz began her report. 'Himself hasn't been to the mill yet, but he's been to Spar and bought a load of food, mostly sausages, and interrogated Carrie. So that's all around the village. And he was sighted very early this morning running with Munro and he'll no doubt have interrogated him, too. What else? Ah yes. Mrs Appleton is wondering if it would offend you if she went and offered herself to him.'

'Cuts lovely,' said the quiche cutter in an aside to Gillian as Liz paused to search her mind for further revelations.

At this point Laura made an entrance, not a wrinkle in her stark mulberry linen. Silence fell. Laura was not discomposed: she expected to receive respectful attention wherever she went. She had come, apparently, on a tour of inspection. She stalked around the loaded tables looking for faults. She took a knife and cut off a minute corner of quiche and nibbled it critically, held in the tips of her enamelled nails.

'Who,' she asked as she nibbled, 'are you dissecting?'

'The new monarch of the glen,' answered Liz. She disliked Laura.

'Ah,' said Laura. 'Major Iain Hampshire.'

'Is there any more butter, Ivy?'

The ladies resumed their labours.

'Are his intentions known yet?' pursued Laura. Her voice was deep and well modulated, in keeping with her other physical perfections. Her character, however, as her friends and relations well knew, was not so perfect. There was nothing wrong with her steel-trap intellect, though, and it occurred to Gillian that if anyone could help put the mill back on the map Laura could.

Listening with half an ear to Liz and Laura exchanging hostile civilities she thought about this. Laura took after her mother who, whatever else she might have been, was a first class business-woman. Laura ought to have been put in charge of the mill when she left the London School of

Economics, Gillian knew. It had been her life-long ambition to follow in her long-dead mother's footsteps and revive tradition. Her mother's family, the Halls, had managed and worked at the mill for more generations than Falconers had owned it. Laura's mother had managed it brilliantly until shortly before Laura was born.

In fact it was Laura's birth that had caused the link to be broken as her mother had driven herself to her death in a violent rage a few weeks afterwards when she discovered that a new manager, an outsider, had been installed at the mill in her absence and that she was now expected to stay at home, bring up her child and not go out to work again. Her volatile family blamed Giles Falconer entirely for her death and tried to claim Laura. But Giles had had enough of the Hall temperament. Laura was sent to friends at the Manor House in a neighbouring village to be looked after by the old nanny there. And by Victoria, the daughter of the house.

Victoria brought Laura back to Falcon Park when she married Giles Falconer – far too soon after Jessica's death for the Halls' liking. The breach between the families became almost total and now, twenty-seven years later, only one Hall, a cousin of Laura's, worked at the run-down mill.

Yes, decided Gillian, with inexplicable reluctance, Laura was the one to lead the mill back uphill again. It had been going steadily downhill since Jessica's exit. Recession had all but put paid to it – hence the massive loan her father had arranged with Hampshire Holdings. But now it could and should be saved – by Laura. And by Major Iain Hampshire. Great Bowland was due for a bit of prosperity. The mill must provide it.

Liz walked over to a window to check progress out on the pitch. 'They've put their demon bowler in again,' she remarked. 'They must be wanting their tea.'

Laura went over to another window. She appeared to be brooding about something. Was it a past wrong, wondered Gillian, watching her? If so, which? As Reg was batting, was she remembering bitterly how Liz had snatched him from her clutches and married him five years ago? Or was she reliving the violent resentment and frustration of those terrible weeks six years ago when Falcon Park rang daily with her screamings and rantings at their father?

If he hadn't been so adamant about keeping Laura out of the mill, Gillian thought (not for the first time), things would have turned out quite differently. The mill would have kept going in a higher gear; there would have been no desperate involvement with Hampshire Holdings; no massive loan; no seizure of the mill and Falcon Park. Her mother would still be living with her father and she, Gillian, would by now have been married to Robin. On the other hand, Laura would not now have owned a business consultancy, a rest home, half a leisure complex and goodness knows what else, not to mention the Elizabethan rectory she lived in.

And Iain Hampshire would now be recuperating somewhere else, unaware of their existence. Her fingers touched the bruises on her neck.

'Now look what's happened!' she heard Liz exclaim. 'The cheeky thing's gone and bowled my Reg out! Mind your back, Laura – here they come.'

Gillian moved over to the urn to help Alice the village matriarch, wife of Sam the blacksmith, dispense tea. Amid the growing uproar as wave after wave of players and supporters entered the pavilion, Gillian's thoughts continued to weave patterns. Yes, Laura was definitely the one Iain should be interrogating and, by now, she thought cynically, Laura would no doubt be thinking so too. There was no need at all to trouble herself about it. As sure as night follows day, Laura's and Iain's paths were about to cross – immediately if not sooner. Laura would see to that herself: then they would interrogate each other – probably in great depth. After that anything could happen.

One of the first things that would happen, Gillian told herself sourly, pouring milk into a row of cups and smiling sweetly at Old Jem, Gracemire's bull-keeper, (who was helping himself to a great many spoonfuls of sugar) was that Laura would get her hooks into Iain as soon as their business dealings were under way and drag him into her fast social life for the rest of his leave – sick or otherwise. They would not be seeing much of him at Gracemire Farm in the near future: that was for sure.

When the last cup had been filled Gillian released herself from duty and found a plate. She was not particularly hungry and would find swallowing painful but she chose a few sandwiches and worked her way through the mob to where she could see her father and Munro in conversation. He finished what he was saying to Munro and came to meet her.

'There you are, darling. Come outside. I have news for you.'

*****

The pavilion was nearly deserted, the players making their way out onto the pitch again, when a shadow fell across the threshold. Laura had come back. With her, his head bent courteously to her vehement undertones, was Major Iain Hampshire.

'Doesn't waste much time, does she,' muttered Liz.

Laura's blue eyes left her companion for a moment and rested on Gillian's shirt. She broke off what she was saying then resumed with renewed animation. Gillian and Liz caught one word: acorns.

'Trust her,' said Liz disgustedly in an undertone to Gillian. Out loud she said: 'Do you want feeding, Iain? There's just this one bit of quiche left. We were keeping it hidden for Sam but he's eaten someone else's.

Laura and Iain spoke together: 'He's had tea with us,' and: 'Yes, thanks,' they said. They looked at each other for a moment, his face expressionless, hers a mask of bitterness and inner turmoil, even about so small a matter.

'He took the portion of quiche, lifted it off its plate and bit into it. 'Very good,' he pronounced.

'Gillian made it,' said Liz gleefully, looking Laura up and down. Laura drew in her breath with a hiss of temper.

Gillian could not stand it. She went off towards the door, ostensibly to watch play.

'Gillian…' his voice arrested her.

'Yes, Major Hampshire?' Who had asked him to use her Christian name?

'Iain,' he corrected. 'Will you have dinner with me at the Grange tomorrow?'

'What are you arranging for tomorrow?' interrupted Laura. 'I was going to suggest you come to me for dinner tomorrow. I'm convinced I can help you. I already have the idea I was telling you about. I could work out the details tonight – recruiting, marketing, and so on – and we could discuss it properly after dinner.'

'What about it, Gillian?' he asked, indicating that the invitation was assumed to include her as well.

Gillian was appalled. She was used to Laura's overbearing ways and occasional boorishness but was quite unprepared for his way of coping with them.

Liz had joined them, determined not to miss anything and to add her mite if possible. Her unselfconscious blue eyes sparkled up at them.

'Gillian goes to church on Sunday evenings,' said Laura with finality.

Iain was regarding Gillian steadily. 'What time does the service finish?'

'Half past seven but I'll not come to dinner, thank you Laura. I have to…'

'Oh come if you want to,' said Laura impatiently. 'You can talk to Dad. Catch up on each other's news.'

In another room, added Gillian silently for her. 'He's told me the news,' she said out loud. 'I can't come anyway because…'

'Do you go to church, Iain?' asked Liz. 'You go on church parades a lot in the army, don't you? You should try ours. Gillian raves about it. Alice sings. The choir's good. The organ's good and the vicar's very funny. That's him bowling now. Gillian tells us about his sermons every Monday. I keep meaning to go myself, but we're pushed on Sundays.'

'That's settled then,' cut in Laura, ignoring Liz. 'I'll explain how to get there. Follow the signposts to Lancaster until you get to Galgate…' Her directions continued until Lance Drysdale lounged in, complaining plaintively about being left to do all the clearing up after their picnic.

Liz dragged Gillian outside. 'Let's go and watch Munro bowling,' she said for the benefit of the others. 'Let the silly bat drag him off to her lair,' she continued once they were out of earshot. 'He may as well get her full measure. He's not as daft as he looks you can tell. Anyway, Uncle Giles'll be around so she'll not be able to throw her knickers over the windmill all that easily.'

'Liz,' said Gillian. 'It's not for me to let, or not let Laura drag him off to her lair or do anything else to him that takes her fancy. All he did was come home with me and try to murder me. That's all. I have no proprietorial rights over him – or Laura – whatsoever. And, unlovely though he is, I wouldn't say he looks daft. Nor would I call what Laura wears knickers.'

'Your throat must be feeling a lot better.'

'It is, thank you. I'm going back in now they've gone.'

'Shall I come and help?' offered Liz, watching Munro tearing down the field.

'I'm not going to do that much: just collect our own plates and so on. Someone else can shift the debris. Have you the Land Rover keys?'

Liz threw them to her.

*****

On her third trip to the Land Rover the carton she was carrying was lifted out of her arms.

'Do you always do all the work?' enquired a disapproving voice. 'This is heavy.'

'They're good solid plates. They need to be.'

'I still want to take you out to dinner,' Iain said next, the carton safely bestowed.

After all – why not? Laura had not as yet gained exclusive rights. 'Thank you. I'm free most evenings.'

'Except Sundays. Who is Alice and what's so special about her?'

'Alice is special in lots of ways and so is Sam. She's his wife.'

'Sam? Ah – yes. Your bodyguard.'

Gillian let this pass. 'Her own voice is out of this world but if you really want the hairs on the back of your neck to rise up and shivers go up and down your spine you should hear her imitating Clara Butt.'

'Clara Butt. That rings a faint bell.'

'There was nothing faint about that bell. They said you could hear her from France on a clear day.'

'Useful.'

'She's been dead ages, of course. Sam got a set of her records at the saleroom about forty years ago. They cost five shillings. They are so old you have to lift the needle on and off manually. They're seventy-eights and weigh a ton. They're practically flat now – I mean smooth. Obviously they were flat to start with. Well, fairly. Alice still plays them all the time, perfecting her technique. They've taped them too, ready for when they give up the ghost altogether.'

This was the longest speech he had so far heard from her. He eyed her curiously as she got behind the wheel. He got in beside her. It went through his mind, as it had through Lance Drysdale's earlier, that she and Laura must have had very different mothers.

As if his thoughts had conjured her up, Laura's Porsche came suddenly out of another gateway from the cricket field, turned towards them and screeched to a stop just in time. The expressive face behind the wheel registered its owner's feelings as she recognised the Land Rover's occupants. Lance Drysdale appeared to be remonstrating with her – successfully evidently as, after a few moments struggle with herself, she decided to give way and reversed back into the field to let them pass. All except Laura saluted gravely when this manoeuvre was complete.

Gillian waited for her passenger to make some remark about her sister. But he had lapsed into a thoughtful silence.

She could keep silent too, she decided. The silence continued until they were nearly at the farm. She drew onto the verge to let a lost motorist squeeze by, deciding how to word what she was going to say next.

'If you want to know about the mill, Laura's your man,' she produced as the car vanished.

A powerful motorcycle was now roaring by. He waited until the sound of it had died away before saying, irrelevantly she thought: 'There's something I've noticed about the natives hereabouts.'

'Which is?'

'They have the oddest ideas about gender. Only this morning I distinctly heard Liz tell Ozymandias he was a good girl.'

'Ozymandias is a she-cat. Shouldn't she be? Is Ozymandias male? I just thought it was the *in* name for cats nowadays and was genderless – like Puss or Topsy or…'

'When I was at school we were definitely informed that he was King of Kings. We were made to learn a poem about him.'

'I wonder if Liz knows? Mind you, she probably wouldn't care anyway. Come to think of it Mog's a he-cat and the Mog he's named after was a Pendle witch. She was going to call Ozymandias after another one – Demdyke – then she read a book and there was a cat in it called Ozymandias. It took her fancy.'

Austin's sheepdogs took no notice of the Land Rover when it swept into the yard with a flourish, pulled up, reversed in an arc and arrived, neatly positioned, its back a foot or two from the kitchen door. When the dogs realised the familiar vehicle was a Trojan Horse containing an alien, an appalled uproar broke out. Gillian knew it would die down after the first outburst. She opened the door into the kitchen and started unloading.

Her assistant's silence resumed as he worked with her and continued after the dogs had gone quiet. She was still waiting for some reaction, some comment at least, about Laura and the mill. Then glancing at him she noticed a drained grey look about him. She straightened up from the dishwasher, Laura and the mill forgotten.

'You're not going to fall asleep again, are you?'

'Of course not.'

Her mind went back to that scene in the cottage. His own words after the attack came back to her. 'For goodness' sake sit down before you fall down,' she said, deliberately sounding unsympathetic. See how he liked being bossed around!

The brief flash in his eyes told her that he knew his words were being thrown back at him. His eyelids were nearly closed. She felt quite alarmed. He really would have to sit down. An idea came to her. What was that other thing he'd said? Something about not touching her until his scars were healed. (And they'd see about that when the time came!) In the meantime, if she approached him, would he move away to avoid contact?

'I don't want to have to catch you, or even touch you with these hands,' she said in the curt tones he had used when saying the same words to her two or three hours ago. She took a step towards him holding out her hands for inspection, their nails short and unpolished, a small blue plaster covering a minor injury on the left palm at the base of her index finger. He stared at it as if fascinated, only dragging his eyes away when she came another step nearer.

She took a third step, slightly to the right, which brought her very close to him. His weary eyes scanned the flawless determined face, its green eyes watchful and very steady. Insensibly, he turned slightly. He only needed to move one step backwards, she judged, and he should land in the rocker if she gave him a good push. She would give him one last chance.

'Do as you're told, Major, or I'll push you down.' Her voice rang cheerfully in the quiet room.

'Ma'am,' he muttered, subsiding into the chair. It rocked backwards to accommodate his long body and became still. He fell asleep.

A frown appeared on her face. She stood for a while, her hands on her hips, watching him. If she were one of his well-wishers, which of course she was not – not that she was now actively an ill-wisher either… Indeed she had possibly let herself soften up towards him during the course of this long strange day. (Odd that being seized by the throat and half-killed by him had not put her off him forever.) If she were a well-wisher… And really, if she were being truthful, she had felt almost at home with him driving here and chatting about cats and opera singers… She had even felt there were thousands of other things they could have gone on to talk to each other about as if already there were some kind of continuity… But that idea was ridiculous to say the least. If she were a well-wisher, a sister say, she would be very very worried about him. It just simply could not be all right to drop asleep like that as if pole-axed. How could he risk driving that peculiar vehicle with all its gadgetry all the way from wherever it was he'd borrowed it from, out of practice as he was. And liable to drop off any moment?

His eyes opened, taking hers by surprise. A smile, the first she had seen, flitted over his face and he winked at her. Then both his eyes closed.

The old clock ticked on unconcerned. Gradually her breathing returned to normal. That smile! She must be going gaga.

Come along, Gillian, she told herself in her mother's firm voice. Finish your jobs then off you go.

FOUR

Strangely Gillian slept well. "Sleep that knits up the ravell'd sleave of care," she mused, lying there, warm and relaxed.

It was Sunday. She could lie there all day if she felt like it. She asked herself what she usually did on Sunday? The events of the last couple of days appeared to have disorientated her somewhat. She must apply her mind to life's normal littlenesses. For instance, she could get up and mow the back lawn, possibly for the last time this year. And she really ought to make a start on altering last year's winter clothes. She could not really afford new ones to fit her new gratifyingly slim shape. The afternoon would, as usual, be taken up with designing.

Jasper interrupted her thoughts at this point by uttering the quiet token barks he used to convey the news that someone known and acceptable had come.

Munro? Gillian went in her demurely yoked nightdress to the open window, shivering slightly at the distinct autumnal nip in the air. Yes, it was Munro. Who else at this time of day? It was barely seven. The glittering beauty of the morning and the man smote her and caught her breath. His perfect teeth gleamed whitely at her in a smile of pure affection that brought back an instant answering smile. It only took moments to fling off her nightdress and put on a strawberry velvet tracksuit, socks and trainers. Moments later she and Jasper had joined Munro at the corner of the church railings.

They ran side by side along the track opposite Gillian's front door, which bordered the rear of the churchyard. They made a striking contrast with each other, Munro being clad entirely in black. Gillian climbed over the stile at the end of the track. Munro vaulted the sturdy field gate beside it and Jasper squirmed through a gap in the hedge. They set off across the shorn turf beyond in the direction of Falcon Park, a furlong or two away, asleep on the hillside.

Gillian got into her stride, flowing along easily. 'Dad's off to Harrogate,' she reported after a few yards. 'Did he tell you?'

Munro turned around without losing pace and ran along backwards facing her. 'He mentioned it. Is it permanent?'

'Hopefully. Mother needs him.'

'She must be doing well.'

'So well it's running away with her. Old Hall has caught on. People like holding conferences and such there suddenly. She needs a resident Mine Host and who better than Dad? He said something about the extensions she's having done too – something about the building inspector and the Heritage people being sticky, it being a listed building. He should be able to sort that out all right. He took great care of Falcon Park; in fact that was almost all he did, apart from riding a lot and entertaining and going here and there with his cronies. Oh – and looking in at the mill once a week, attending the odd board-meeting…' She broke off, realizing she was sounding not critical exactly but not complimentary either.

Munro, however, having lived and worked at Falcon Park for two years, knew she was not being disloyal, was merely stating facts.

'Not,' she admitted, 'that I was doing anything particularly meaningful myself those days, looking back.'

'And now?'

'Definitely. Feeding hungry working men is very satisfying. Helping Liz make money with the horses is satisfying. Come to think of it, providing the experience and exercise of riding for people without horses is satisfying. What else? I really must do a stock-take next time I've an hour or two to spare.'

'Of what – the pluses and minuses of life now compared with life then?'

'Exactly.'

Gillian now needed all her breath for running. They changed direction, turning right along a bridlepath. Munro was by now running forwards again. He slowed the pace down to a walk.

'Munro,' she said after a short breather. 'Do you think Mum saw all this coming? You did meet her a few times, didn't you, when you drove Dad to Harrogate to visit her so he could drink and not have to drive home?'

'I'm quite sure she saw everything that was coming.'

'So she didn't just leave home because she refused to live on borrowed money. She left to build up a – a *living* for the three of us for when the crash, which Dad didn't imagine would come, finally came.'

'Of course.'

'How blind and thick I was not to see for myself! I was totally devastated when she left. Nothing, *nothing* as frightful ever happened to me ever, either before or since – including getting thrown out of the Park.'

'Naive, perhaps. A bit blind. Not thick – you weren't told everything. So there's a job for you at Harrogate too?'

'Yes.'

He studied her profile for a moment then put a brotherly arm around her shoulders, refraining from probing further. Two joggers pounded past them, puffing short greetings. She looped her arm around his waist and enjoyed his friendly warmth until the path took them round the next bend.

Munro removed his arm and consulted his watch. 'Got your breath back?' He led the way down another path which meandered back to where they had first struck off down the bridlepath. It was all private land around here belonging to Falcon Park but villagers had been free to roam at will for generations.

Today there seemed to be more early dog walkers and joggers about than usual. Noticing this, Gillian deduced that the news of sightings of the returned hero, running early on previous mornings, had brought the curious out of their beds hours before normal time for most of them. Well, she for one was not going to join their ranks. Why was Munro edging her along in a certain direction like an efficient sheepdog? Suspicion had barely formed before it was too late.

They rounded the massive girth of an ancient spreading cedar tree and there he was, waiting for them.

She could see it all now. If she needed final proof that he and Munro were in league, there it was before her. The tracksuit the Major was wearing belonged to Munro. She could identify it by a rather messy repair at the bottom of one leg. Those were her stitches. She had volunteered to mend that tear last Christmas.

'He wants to be seen to be on good terms with you,' Munro was saying. 'News has got round somehow.' He touched her neck. 'The natives are wondering whether to turn ugly.'

Iain heard these words but made no sign of having done so. 'What very odd tracks you leave,' was his first remark.

'Good morning, Major Hampshire,' she said, her tone rebuking his lack of manners.

'Oh, Lord. She's still at it,' he said to Munro.

'Did you waken safely back at the farm?' she asked in a chatty, society hostess voice with a hidden cutting edge. 'Or are they now a cat short? Did Mog jump on your knee?'

'Mog is alive and well. Also Ozymandias.'

'Ozymandias?' repeated Munro, apparently stunned.

'Liz's cat. Liz's *she*-cat,' explained Gillian.

Munro gave a shout of laughter, turned and sprinted off. '"My name is Ozymandias, King of Kings",' they heard him declaim. '"Look on my works, ye Mighty…"' He vanished dramatically into a wisp of mist lingering in a green hollow.

They watched the spot where he had vanished for a few seconds.

'Now that,' said Gillian, 'is what I'd call a splendid exit.'

'He must have had to learn that poem at school too.'

'What – in France?'

'He's *French?*'

'Actually Munro did do a year at Oxford so perhaps…' Her voice trailed away. So he wanted to be seen to be on good terms with her. Right! Stepping back, she took him completely by surprise by turning a perfect cartwheel. Jasper tore around her barking excitedly. 'Race you to that chestnut,' she called out – whether to Iain or to the dog it was not clear. And off she went.

She felt him draw level with her before she saw him. She did not hear him at all. He had caught up with her in long, bounding strides, timing his soft footfalls to coincide with hers to fool her. The three of them arrived at the chestnut together.

When she got her breath back she said: 'At least ten people were looking our way. I can give you their names if you want. Can I go home now?'

'If you mean Falcon Park, yes. I want my breakfast. I'll cook yours too.'

'Of course I don't mean Falcon Park! Falcon Park stopped being home in April. No thank you. I have to get back.'

'Not even you can possibly be working today. Come on – there's no need to look like that. I've hardly had time to tear it apart yet if that's what you're thinking. It's got a bit damp and musty standing empty so long, but it's all right in the kitchen where I live.'

'Do you sleep in there too?' she enquired, allowing herself to be steered a few steps towards her old home. Jasper cavorted about them eagerly.

'No. Nor do I sleep in your father's king-sized. I sleep in what was probably Munro's room.'

'And you wear his clothes.'

He looked down, following her gaze. 'I must get myself a couple of tracksuits.'

'Laura sells them at her gym.'

'Laura has a gym? I thought she was a business consultant.'

'That too. She owns a rest home as well, at Arnside. The gym is half hers. It's a leisure complex. She's into flats now. Or was last time I heard - converting some big old town houses in Lancaster. I wonder if she's involved Dad...'

'He is involved. Laura told me about that. He's good at it, apparently. Keeps the workmen on their toes, turns his hand to quite a lot of the jobs himself. The first house is ready now. Laura has offered me the garden flat. She tells me Falcon Park costs too much to run just for one.'

'Did she tell you what to do with it?'

'She had a few suggestions.'

Gillian barely noticed that by degrees they were drawing nearer to the rear of the mansion. Laura, she was thinking, was an ever-ready fund of suggestions, not to mention home truths and opinions. She herself had suffered a shell-burst of them back in April when Laura had arrived at the Park, a few hours before deadline, and borne their father off with her like a trophy, leaving Gillian with suggestions, home truths and opinions ringing in her ears, topped off with the parting shot that it was no use imagining that she, Laura, could or would support her as well as their father; nor was it any use going crying to her mother as *she* could not afford to support a deadweight either.

'Are your feet hurting?' Iain asked, breaking into her thoughts.

Realising that she had been frowning and silent for several minutes and that quite a distance had been covered during that time, she recollected herself. 'Not at all,' she replied. They were almost at the back door. 'I'm not going into that house!'

'Sure? I don't want to have to carry you over the threshold. There's a very fierce-looking little old lady over there with a dangerous-looking pug. I'm not risking it.'

'Also you've vowed never to touch me,' she reminded him.

'I have,' he agreed. 'I nearly forget it every time you call me Major Hampshire but so far I've managed to refrain from…' He had the back door open now.

She peered inside, memories flooding in. 'Strangling me again?' she murmured. Should she go in, just to see what it felt like? Would there be ghosts? She failed to observe the effect of her words – the spasm that darkened his contused face.

Somehow she was in. Nothing had changed. Mrs. Appleton might come bustling out of the pantry at any moment, crackling with cleanliness, plump with good cooking. She half-expected to see Munro in shirt-sleeves, his feet up on the Aga, reading Chaucer.

'Shall I?'

'No,' he said. 'I will. It gives me a kick to cook at high speed. If you know where there's a squeezer you could empty one of these grapefruit for me. Suit yourself what you do with the other one. I like mine squeezed but not chilled.'

She knew where the squeezer would be; might as well have her grapefruit that way too. She got out two glasses, which she washed first, not trusting them after their long disuse. The water was very hot. He had evidently fathomed the somewhat eccentric plumbing. Had he filled the pool she wondered? If so, had he cleaned it out first? The Aga, she noticed, he had not lit. She took his glass over to him where he already had the frying pan getting hot on the electric hob – too hot in her opinion. The fat seemed all right, she saw, half expecting it to be full of black bits.

'I sieved it last night,' he said, reading her thoughts. 'I've just got it to its peak of maturity.' A loud crackling broke out as he arranged several rashers of bacon neatly in the large pan.

'If I put the grill on,' she suggested, 'the plates would warm.'

'So they would. They're in the dishwasher. I store them there.'

'Don't you use it, then?'

'I switched it on yesterday and will no doubt do so again tomorrow.'

'And the clean things get washed again along with the dirty ones. I see. Well, I suppose there's no harm in that. What if you want a plate while it's going?'

'It will be a long time before I run out of plates – or the QEII, if it should happen to come and moor up outside.'

'That was Mum. She couldn't resist sales. Auction sales that is. Never came home without a boot-load of Rockingham, Doulton… You name it.'

'She started an hotel though didn't she? Why didn't she take it with her?'

'She did. She did. What's left here are the dregs.'

'Why didn't you go with her? With your cooking talents… *ouch!*'

'I admit I now make a lovely hotpot. I couldn't then. I had no talents at all then. No useful ones. If you could just bring yourself to turn it down a little bit you'd not get as spat at.'

'True. But just look at it – thundering along!'

'It'll burst into flames in a minute.'

'It did that yesterday morning. It was very annoying. I had to start again with new fat and the old lot was just getting ripe. *Blast!*'

She placed two plates under the grill and set it to her liking. Then she retreated to a safe distance, sipping her tart drink. She wanted to know all sorts of things about how he had settled in. Better wait until he'd coped with the eggs though as he had four lined up there. She herself could cook four eggs in one pan without letting them collide but the technique had taken weeks to perfect. He seemed to be managing with the bacon still in the pan, heaped to one side. Ah – he was doing them in twos. Much safer and simpler.

When her plate reached the table she saw that the two eggs had not merely collided: they had managed a complete merger. They looked like one huge double-yolked egg. The whole meal was absolutely delicious. The best meal she had ever tasted in her whole life. Afterwards they had several slices of fried bread to fill up. His coffee was good, too.

Jasper wandered in and flopped down under the table. A silence of contentment descended. He was sinking lower and lower in his chair, his eyes nearly closed.

'Are you going off again?' she asked, sitting up anxiously after three or four minutes.

'Probably,' he murmured. 'Damn pills.'

'*Pills?* What are you taking for Heaven's sake?'

'Something the medic's trying out…' His voice trailed away.

'You mean he's *experimenting* on you?'

'They've tried them out on…tigers…and…jetlag. In quarantine.'

'You can't go to sleep there!' She was standing over him now.

'Not to worry. I've none left.' He yawned, heaving himself out of the chair. 'Go home, Gillian.'

'I will when I've put you to bed.'

'That's very…very…' Another yawn swallowed whatever the end of the sentence might have been. 'Go home,' he managed again.

'Follow me or I'll drag you.'

'Ma'am.'

What a blessing he was using Munro's old room just across the passage, she thought, as he followed her, heavy-footed.

A great deal of sunshine was pouring in through the east window. The three-quarter bed had a royal blue sheet stretched taut over it and one pillow in clean white linen. An enormous duvet was draped over a chair by the window. He fell on the bed with a sigh.

'Jet-lagged tigers indeed!' she said. 'If I were your…'

'My?'

'Mother – I wouldn't let them use you as a guineapig.'

'You can be my surro…surrog…' He gave up.

She bent over him. Was that a strip of grey glinting between his eyelids?

Suddenly the eyes opened. He reached out and grasped her head. She felt one moment of blind panic as her head was pulled down. Then he kissed her lips, deliberately, once. And let her go.

'I didn't do that, Mother,' he slurred. His eyes closed. He was fast asleep.

It was quite a large room and not warm in spite of the sun. What was the best thing to do? In the end she gathered up the duvet and lowered it by degrees over him, ready to jump backwards if he moved. She debated whether to open the mullioned window a bit. There weren't likely to be any intruders and he would no doubt rouse up (and how!) if anyone, a member of the Press, say, were foolish enough to try and get through it. She opened it about four inches then arranged one of the curtains so that sunlight did not fall across his face.

*****

The flowers had been removed from the hearth and a fire laid, Gillian saw, as soon as she and Jasper got back to her cottage. That meant that her friend, Brenda, had been in. She must have called to bring Gillian the next thing she noticed, which was last evening's paper, lying there on a chair, and decided to do a few jobs while she was here.

Gillian put a match to the fire and remained on her knees in front of it. She would just glance through that paper, she thought, and see what rubbish was in it, if any, about the man who had just addressed her as Mother and told her to go home. There must be something about him in it – Brenda didn't ordinarily bring her newspapers to read. She shook it open and scanned the pages quickly. There did not seem to be anything. She folded it back to the front page and started again.

Her attention was caught by a picture which her eyes had passed without interest before of a man so unfairly handsome he could only be a film star or some such. It couldn't be... She reached out and pulled her angled draughtsman's lamp down by its shade and switched it on. After a long scrutiny she had to let herself believe it. The bone structure fitted both that handsome face, strong-fleshed and alert, lit up before her now, and the cadaverous, damaged, sleeping one she had put in the shade by drawing a curtain half an hour ago. It was several minutes before she began to read.

Yesterday's morning papers had dealt entirely with news of the missing men's return; their exploits and misadventures; the implications of what they had discovered. The evening papers had had more time to delve into the men's backgrounds. The one Gillian held, while her new fire was dying for want of attention, was a Lancashire daily and had therefore concentrated its beam on the man who had chosen to base himself in this area rather than join his family for his "well deserved recovery leave" as the journalist who had written the long article put it.

A despairing rustle in the hearth drew her abstracted attention. She dropped the paper, struck another match and applied it to the paper and sticks where the puny flames had not reached.

What a homecoming! Liz had pointed that out to her yesterday, she remembered, but yesterday she had not been prepared to trouble herself with wondering what he had had to face up to immediately following his other ordeals.

'Out of the frying-pan, in fact,' she said to the fire.

Jasper thumped his tail. Gillian inserted the nose of the bellows into the heart of the fire and puffed delicately. Answering flames sprang up and set about their business.

What was the name again of the man Iain's fiancée had married? She abandoned the bellows and picked up the paper. Her hand began to shake. Her eyes flew down the column. He surely could not be *that* Parker! Not the Parker who had stormed in on them the night before they left the Park, his eyes gleaming in mad triumph, who had gone through their home, throwing open cupboards and wardrobes, foam at the corners of his mouth. Until her father knocked him down on the landing, dragged him downstairs by his collar and pushed him ungently through the ancient front door, which closed behind him with a solid bang, which Gillian still occasionally heard in her dreams.

No – Iain's fiancée had not married that Parker. She had married his son. Parker senior was now, Gillian read, residing in a mental home. A description followed of the havoc he had caused when he had seized the reins of Hampshire Holdings during the brief period of confusion following the death of his brother-in-law, Iain's father.

That made Parker Junior Iain's cousin, Gillian mused. And Miss Marianna Merrivale had married him. She had been engaged to Iain, been on the point of marrying him when he'd been posted off to South America. She had waited less than three months to see if he was still alive after the men had been reported missing. She had abandoned him. Here was an excellent photograph of her: a laughing, mischievous looking girl, undoubtedly a beauty, who would probably have kept the Major happy and stimulated, if he had remained there beside her helping to generate the continual excitement her expressive face seemed to be demanding.

The rest of the article was on an inside page. Gillian found it and read the promise made by the paper to its readers that it would do its best to solve the mystery of why Falcon Mill and Falcon Park, Great Bowland, had been the target for Parker's special destructive attention and what the new head of Hampshire Holdings intended to do about its precarious future now he was fixed in the area for the duration of his leave.

*****

Half an hour later Brenda looked in to see if Gillian wanted, as she sometimes did, to come with her and her husband, Bob, on their usual Sunday lunchtime rounds of the local pubs.

'Is that the time?' asked Gillian, astonished.

'Saw it, did you? That bit about Himself.'

'*Himself?* Is that what everyone's calling him?'

'Some. We're off to Chipping first today. Our Beatie wants a lift. Are you coming?'

'Better not. I haven't got going yet.'

'We'll be off then. I'll fetch the Sundays along later when Herself's done with them. There's a bit more about him in them.' "Herself" was Brenda's mother-in-law with whom she lived in a state of uneasy truce three doors down from Gillian's cottage. Brenda was Sam and Alice's youngest child. She and Gillian had become close friends soon after Gillian moved into Church Row.

After that Gillian applied herself to her normal Sunday pursuits. She washed her hair and left it to dry naturally as she settled down at her drawing board.

From time to time she let Jasper in and out and put coal or logs on the fire. Later on she mowed the lawn, ate a few jam sandwiches and, a few minutes before half past six, closed her front door behind her. She glanced involuntarily up the fields to the left and saw a large shape leaving the shadows of Falcon Park. So he had got out the Rolls. Was it still taxed? Laura would be pleased. She liked status symbols to be seen parked about her rectory – although that odd-looking jeep would perhaps have rated more highly as a status symbol just now while its driver was such hot news.

Gillian entered her usual pew and knelt down. She remained on her knees longer than usual due to forgetting to get up after the usual half minute. Someone else entering the pew and sitting down brought her back to her surroundings. She rose from her knees and sat down, glancing to see who it was, nearly giving a squeak of surprise when she saw. How could he have got here in that time? What about Laura's dinner? Where had he parked the Rolls? How fit and smart (comparatively) he looked! Those pills must be doing him some good after all.

'Didn't want to miss Dame Clara Butt,' he whispered.

'What about Laura?'

'Rang her up. Told her I couldn't get there till eight. Will I make it?'

She nodded. The choir was filing in, Alice its centrepiece, impressive in a scarlet gown with ivory lace. Everyone stood up.

He knew all the hymns and the Order of Service, using his prayer book only for the psalm, she noticed, adding her well-schooled soprano to his confident baritone. Everyone there knew who he was. The atmosphere acquired a new lift felt by everyone. The hour passed on wings; the sermon made everyone laugh twice and also provided food for thought. And then came the vesper – Lead Me Lord. Affected by the electricity in the air, Alice's contralto voice excelled itself. Everyone left the church bright-eyed and exalted.

In the porch the vicar pounced on Iain. Gillian lingered as he invited Iain to join him and a few others at a clay pigeon shoot on Tuesday. He'd enjoy that, Iain said. He hadn't got his own gun with him but there were about twenty to choose from at the Park. They fixed the time and transport and then the vicar's attention was drawn off by a stout matron with a hoarse voice who had no intention of leaving without bidding the vicar her usual majestic farewell.

The Rolls was parked in front of her cottage taking up most of the road. They walked side by side towards it.

'It should practically be in the bag now,' Gillian remarked.

'Mmm?'

'Your Good Conduct medal.'

He ignored this sally. 'Would you do something for me, Gillian?'

'Sir.' She bowed.

'I've a young chap coming on Tuesday for a few days. My grandfather tells me he's our likeliest bet. Could you persuade your Mrs. Appleton to come and sort things out – catering and so forth – while he's here?'

'She's already wondering whether to offer herself to you. Yes – I'll go and see her. She only lives around the corner.'

'I'll drive you there.'

'Better not. She'll expect you to come in, which could take hours. Heads will roll if you're late for dinner. Not yours – mine and Mrs. Appleton's, for delaying you.'

She left him standing by the superb silver-grey car. They looked made for each other, she thought. Laura would think so too.

FIVE

'Never mind bad eggs,' said Liz, breaking a fresh one into a saucer. 'I've had a word with the hens recently about that.' She sniffed at the egg and tipped it into Gillian's batter. '*Tell* me!'

So Gillian gave her a more or less factual version of yesterday, going into quite a lot of detail about other things she had done too, to tease her.

'Yes, well – I don't particularly want to know what Jasper had for dinner. What I want to know is: do you definitely fancy him?'

Her voice had risen to compete with the noise Gillian was now making with the whisk. They did not know Austin had come in until he was right up to them. 'Who – me?' he asked.

'Not today,' said Gillian, opening the range oven door and recoiling at the blast of heat.

'I'll do that,' he said, getting the dripping tins out for her. The fat in them was sizzling. She ladled in the batter, finally tipping up the bowl to get the last drop out. Austin put the tins back in the bottom of the oven.

'That fire's a bit too frisky,' Gillian remarked. 'Could you bank it down a bit or everything'll be overdone before I get back.'

Austin did this and also drove Liz's Volvo out of its garage for Gillian, while she went to find the cheque book and other documents she would need at the trade market. He would dearly have liked to have driven off to Lancaster with her but he had work to do. She waved to him as she drove out of the yard, leaving him disconsolate, a dog on either side of him. Really, she thought, he was a nice man, even if he was over-sexed and drank too much. She could quite see what the village maidens saw in him. Odd that she herself had no difficulty in resisting the definite pull he possessed, especially as it was trained so fiercely in her direction. Perhaps it was his strong family likeness to

Laura, whose cousin he was. Or perhaps there was something wrong with her.

'"Tell me where is fancy bred. Or in the heart or in the head?"' she sang.

*****

Driving back into Great Bowland shortly before twelve Gillian looked across the valley towards the mill, nestling in its fold of green hillside. That looked like Laura's Porsche glinting in the sun, parked to the side of it.

'Here we go,' she said, not respectfully, under her breath.

Sam was already ladling out broth when she arrived in the kitchen and someone had taken one of the casseroles of stew out of the oven and two of the Yorkshire puddings. Gillian left everything in the car until later except for the frozen goods, which she put away in the freezer. Old Jem (having removed his teeth first) was already helping himself to stew and Austin was cutting up Yorkshire puddings into neat triangles. Gillian left them to it and went off to make a lot of custard.

Liz sidled in as she was withdrawing a large roly-poly pudding from the electric oven. 'Perfect,' she said, poking it. 'Gillian…'

Gillian glanced up then looked more sharply at her cousin. 'What?' she enquired suspiciously. She began cutting up the long roll of suet pastry, letting out puffs of steam and hot jam.

'I did mention, didn't I,' said Liz airily, 'that I've invited Iain to lunch again.'

'You've what?'

'He's going to pay the same as our men do, he says.'

'When's he coming?'

'Every day.'

'Liz! What *time's* he coming?'

'Second sitting I should think.'

'Watch this milk, will you. I'd better rescue some of that stew.' She did this in the nick of time, putting the casserole back in the range.

The fire was exactly right: everything would keep warm; nothing would overcook. She was just wiping down the table after the last man from the first sitting had left when the jeep came into the yard. It was twenty to one. Then there he was, standing to attention in front of her.

'Thanks, Gillian. It's all fixed. Mrs. Appleton phoned me this morning.'

The others carried on with exaggerated unconcern: Christine at the sink, washing her hands, Reg idly leafing through a circular, Liz poking about in the broth pan with a ladle. Christine began bringing knives, forks and spoons across. Recalled to her duties, Gillian hurried to get the soup bowls as Liz filled them.

'Have you had a good morning, Iain?' enquired Liz, taking her place and waving him to the same place he had occupied on Saturday.

'Enlightening, certainly.'

'And what's the verdict?'

'Laura has almost convinced me there's potential.'

Liz grimaced, but said, albeit grudgingly: 'She'll know if anyone does. Knows the mill, knows all the workers, knows everyone else round here, knows how many beans make five.'

'Gillian said on Saturday that Laura was my man.'

'Gillian said *what?*' Liz looked at Gillian, revolted.

They all glanced out of the window as a car swished into the yard.

'Whoops! Fasten your seat belts. It's Herself in person,' said Liz, adding in an audible undertone: 'Mother-bloody-Demdyke.'

Laura stood framed in the doorway, pulsating with annoyance. 'Look Iain,' she said without preamble. 'There's absolutely no need to come here to eat. I told you I'd had a hamper put up this morning. I intended that we should have a working lunch. I have to be at Arnside at three. We've got to get this thing settled.'

'Sorry Laura,' said Iain, at once. 'I didn't realise you were inviting me to share your lunch when you told me about the hamper. I mentioned last night, if you remember, that Liz suggested on Saturday that I had lunch here until I'm organised.'

His quiet voice, at variance with her angry one, had its effect on her. After a moment's struggle, she came towards the table. Gillian pulled out a chair at the foot of the table for her.

'Do you still like custard, Laura?' she asked. Receiving no answer, she poured a generous helping into a bowl and handed her sister a spoon. Laura examined the spoon with distaste then started to consume the custard while everyone else carried on with their broth.

'Tell us more about your plans, Iain,' urged Liz, knowing it would probably annoy Laura to hear that Iain had been discussing plans with anyone but her.

Laura's face darkened. Gillian cut a slice of jam roly-poly and transferred it to Laura's dish, adding more custard. She served stew to everyone else, leaving them to help themselves from the various hot serving dishes already on the table.

'Tentatively speaking,' said Iain, 'Our plans are two-pronged. Prong One is obviously to get more orders going through and build up the workforce. That's Nesbit's department.'

'Is Nesbit the miracle worker who's coming this afternoon?' asked Gillian, pushing a jug of gravy towards him.

Laura stopped eating for a moment, arrested by this evidence that Gillian was so up to date with information.

'From my grandfather's description. I haven't met him yet. All I know about him so far is that he's young, he calls himself the assistant company secretary, he goes from mill to mill listening and has an unerring knack, according to Grandad, of homing in on things like discrepancies, waste of any kind, incongruities, trouble makers, et cetera. After which things suddenly get done about it, apparently without any visible effort on his part. Parker tried to sack him, of course, but he took no notice.'

He looked directly at Gillian as he said the last sentence. She stared back at him, resentment stirring. What was he thinking? That she and her father shouldn't have taken any notice of Parker either? Should have stayed put at Falcon Park, ignoring the bailiffs and the pressures put on them to go quietly, not to mention the reasons behind their departure?

She began clearing away empty plates, annoyance warring with hope for the village that his earlier words had raised. She wielded a knife along the length of the second jam roly-poly, eyeing him bodingly between slashes. She would put him right before he was much older. He watched, an answering glint in his eye.

'There's some stew left if you want it, Laura,' she said, still eyeing him.

Laura turned her head away in disgust. Her sister found a plate, onto which she tipped the remainder of the stew. Christine supplied clean cutlery then went back to the horses. Liz watched with fascination as Laura made short work of the stew, reaching out and helping herself to the last two pieces of Yorkshire pudding and using the one remaining slice of bread to mop up the gravy left on her plate – daintily with a knife and fork. 'What's Prong Two?' asked Liz faintly.

'Laura will tell you about Prong Two,' said Iain.

'Leave her alone. She's busy.'

'So she is.' He proceeded forthwith, between mouthfuls of pudding, to tell them of Laura's plans for diversification; for the launch of a new "Bowland Forest" range of fabrics and other spin-offs, not necessarily textile, which could eventually involve every man, woman and child in the village who was not already in employment.

'A co-operative?' asked Reg, holding out his dish for a second helping.

'Now that…' Iain lapsed into silence, finishing his sweet off very quickly as he turned the idea over.

As if programmed, Liz rose from her seat and moved over to the hob. She ladled broth into a warm soup-dish and put it in front of Laura who, at that moment, had just wiped her plate clean of its last spot of gravy. Laura seized a spoon.

Reg heaved himself to his feet when Laura had at last finished her back-to-front meal. Liz apologised to her for the absence of hors d'oeuvres to finish off with. Ignoring this, Laura got to her feet. 'If you're ready, Iain. *Get away, cat!*' Ozymandias had strolled in and with typical bad judgement had chosen Laura's leg to rub up against.

'Have some coffee, Laura,' said Reg from the rocker by the fire. He looked sympathetically at Iain, knowing how he would have liked to have taken possession of the other rocking chair.

'No thank you. There simply isn't time.' Laura assumed the manner of an honoured guest, departing graciously. 'Everything was simply delicious, Gillian. We enjoyed it. Thank you.'

Gillian raised one eyebrow at the proprietorial "we".

'Did Mrs. Appleton teach you how to cook?' murmured Iain, hopefully, as he passed her – a much more acceptable compliment.

Liz and Gillian watched through the window as the Porsche and the jeep left the yard.

'She's still a frightful driver, I see,' remarked Liz.

'Like her mother was. I wouldn't want Laura to get killed that way too, though.'

'We'll have to think of some other way then. Better wait till after she's launched the village I suppose.'

'Liz!'

'I bet you she turns up here again tomorrow – if he does that is. Perhaps he won't now he's got Mrs. Appleton.'

'We'll just have to wait and see. Or not see as the case may be. Maybe we'll not see much of either of them from now on. We might never see the miracle worker at all. They're going to be very busy by the sound of it.'

'It'll not be Laura's fault if they're not.'

'I wonder what she's got planned for the three of them tonight?'

'Something, no doubt. Her plans won't necessarily come off though. You can tell he'll not push around all that easily. If at all.'

*****

And so it proved. Whatever Laura had planned otherwise, there came a brief double-rap on Gillian's front door shortly before nine that evening. Before she had time to get to her feet the door opened. And there he was.

'Sorry to barge in,' he said when he could make himself heard over Jasper's greetings. 'It's another of those little things that give me a kick at the moment – barging about, opening… What on earth's going on up there?' His eyes were scanning the ceiling from which rhythmic crashing sounds were coming.

'That's Brenda.'

'What on earth's Brenda doing?'

The crashing stopped for a moment and Brenda's voice could be heard, swearing.

'I've heard that voice somewhere. Not swearing. I've got it! Dame Clara Butt.'

'Son of.'

'There you go again.'

'She's Alice and Sam's youngest. They have ten children. Brenda's husband's on nights, which is why she's round here. Her mother-in-law won't let her enjoy herself keeping house at home.'

'Is that what she's doing up there – housekeeping?'

'At the moment she's knitting. Are you going to sit here?' She indicated the other armchair.

'The more I see you the more it gets like Alice Through the Looking Glass. No – I'll sit here.' He sat down on the saddle-stool.

'Are you cold?'

This was evidently taken as a pleasantry that needed no answer. He lowered himself onto the stool. Silence fell apart from the crackling of the fire he was now staring into and the rhythmic clashing sounds of the knitting machine in the spare bedroom.

It is the duty of a hostess, Gillian heard her mother's voice saying in her head, to put her guests at ease. She looked enquiringly at her unbidden guest, feeling no urge to put him at his ease. Indeed, looking at him, he already was at ease. More – he looked at home. Perhaps he thought this cottage had belonged to her family and now, therefore, belonged to Hampshire Holdings.

Well - it didn't belong to Hampshire Holdings. Nor, to be strictly accurate, did it belong to her either – yet. Uncle Matt (Liz's father) was supposed to be selling it to her. But he was notoriously difficult to part from his property. He preferred acquiring property and had readily paid fabulous sums into her building society account for Columbine, and the Range Rover she had sold to him when her old life came to an end last Easter. And there that money still was, waiting for the conveyancing of the cottage to her to be put in hand.

She did not see why she should go into any of these details with her visitor, though. Let him find out for himself what he did and didn't own.

As he seemed in no hurry to speak she would remain silent also. She stood up and moved behind him for no particular reason other than that she felt she had remained long enough poised waiting to hear his reason, if any, for coming. Immediately he whipped around to face her, almost overturning the heavy stool as he half rose to his feet.

'Sorry,' he said, subsiding. 'Sorry.'

She remained behind him, slightly to his left, recovering from this manifestation, this *second* manifestation, that part of him was still back in the jungle, tuned in to danger, real or imagined. He did not attempt to explain. Nor did he let himself face her again although she could tell he was tense and willing her to move from behind him. A coal fell out of the fire and lay smoking in the hearth. He leaned forward to toss it back into the fire. He heard her gasp and straightened up instantly, his free hand whipping behind him to tug down his tracksuit top. But it was too late. She had seen some exposed back. Now he spoke…

'About Parker,' he began. 'I had a long session with your father last night.' He stopped, knowing she was not listening to him. 'Gillian, may I have your attention, please.'

She steeled herself and crept towards him. Her hand reached out to lift up the black silky material. But he was too quick. He leapt to his feet and turned to face her.

'No, Gillian. You are not going to…be exposed to my back.'

For a moment he held her steady, darkly fringed green gaze. His expression softened slightly as he took in the determined line of her lovely mouth. 'In a few months – when I look less like an escapee from a horror film…' He broke off to move back sharply to evade her hand, reaching for the tab of the zip at his throat. 'Miss Falconer, I have to tell you that it is unbecoming conduct to try and undress your visitors within minutes of arrival! And don't look at me like that, please, or I'll…'

'What's that you've got in your pocket?' she interrupted.

'What? A handkerchief, of course.'

'It's a tin of ointment. May I see it please?'

'You may not. If you would just sit down again I could…'

'Major Hampshire, sit down yourself.'

'After you,' he said politely.

'I'm sending for reinforcements. Brenda was a nurse,' she informed him. She raised her voice: 'BRENDA!'

The sounds from the second bedroom stopped. 'What's up?' came down Brenda's voice.

'Can you come down?'

A few moments later Brenda trod across the threshold.

'Brenda, this is Major Iain Hampshire.'

'Aye, I know. Pleased to meet you.' Brenda held out her hand. He reached out automatically to take it then withdrew at the last moment. Brenda calmly possessed herself of the hand, however, and subjected it to close scrutiny. 'Healing all right,' she commented. 'What was it you wanted, Gillian? Is it brew time?'

'No. I'll brew in a bit,' said Gillian as Brenda half-turned towards the kitchen. 'It's his back. I've seen it. What do you think your father would suggest?' She studied the grim figure before the fire. His narrowed eyes looked coldly down at her for a long moment.

'I can see that you think you've clinched everything,' he said. 'Why I can't imagine. However, Brenda can anoint my back if she can stand the sight of it. It will save me doing my Indian God act for an hour or two.' The tin of ointment was placed with a decided snap on the arm of Gillian's vacated chair. They looked at him expectantly. After a moment he unhurriedly removed the top of his tracksuit. An old-fashioned vest was revealed, shortened by frequent washings, with sleeves down to the elbows, buttoned at the throat. He undid the three buttons. 'You're sure?'

'Get the damned thing off,' said Gillian, irritably, her nerves stretched in anticipation of what else she was about to see. Keeping his eyes fixed on hers and his back towards Brenda he did so.

'Bluddy hell!' There was a pause while Brenda examined the exposed back. 'I thought our Luke's was a mess when he sluthered down that quarry and got his back all ripped up.'

Gillian remained where she was, facing him, looking thoughtfully at the startling muscles on his long, too lean arms. She saw the network of scratches and other lacerations on them and on his wide shoulders and otherwise smooth well-muscled chest. If only she (if she was going to continue to provide his lunches) and Mrs. Appleton could put some weight on him – two stones, say…'

'It's coming on all right, though,' pronounced Brenda at last. 'Except this bit down here. What's in that tin?'

'It's for that bit down there. Mother Nature's taking care of the rest.'

Brenda opened the tin and sniffed at the contents. 'Not much left. Have you got any more?'

'No.'

'I'll get Dad. He'll get something mixed up by tomorrow.'

'I'll go,' said Gillian. 'Where is he?'

Brenda thought a moment. 'He said he was going to look at the bells.' She went to look out of the window towards the church's squat tower. 'There's a light so he's still up there. I'll just nip over. Don't let him get cold.'

'I wonder how she expects me to do that?' wondered Gillian after Brenda went out. 'I could turn you around, bit by bit, I suppose. As on a spit.'

'Are you a ghoul, Miss Falconer?'

Her hand flew towards his bruised face. The room became very still as she stood there, her hand an inch away from his cheek.

'Consider yourself slapped,' she said into the silence. Her hand withdrew.

'Consider yourself retaliated against.'

'Apologise!'

'Sit down, can't you. I apologise. I admit it was a…'

'…nasty…'

'…thing to say.'

'Yes,' she agreed. 'You keep saying – and doing – nasty things to me.' She sat down on the edge of the hearth and folded her arms on her drawn up knees.

'Are you flirting with me, Miss Falconer?'

'*Am* I? Gosh – I didn't think I knew how. Am I any good at it would you say?'

'Do men who look like…'

She waited with a look of expectancy on her face for him to decide how to describe what he thought he looked like. 'The wreck of the Hesperus?' she suggested, with the air of a small child guessing wildly and wrongly at the answer required of it.

'…attract you?'

She appeared to give this question careful thought. 'I don't know yet,' she said judicially. 'I've not met enough to find out. On the other hand, do excessively handsome ones?

Let me see now. There's Austin and there's Munro. There was another handsome face I saw recently, too. I wonder where? But handsomeness doesn't count all that much. After you've got used to seeing it you don't notice it any more. It's the essential Munro-ness of Munro that counts; the essential Major Hampshire-ness of Major… Here they come!'

After the briefest of greetings Sam wasted no time at all. Neither did he hurry himself. He asked Gillian to shine her lamp onto Iain's back, which she did, seeing the back herself for the first time as she did so. Nothing in her sheltered life had prepared her for such a sight but she managed not to faint or exclaim. If her face lost some of its colour no one noticed. Iain sat like a rock, his jaw taut, his hands braced on his knees, staring into the heart of the fire.

'What got at you down here?' Sam asked after a while.

'No idea. It had a couple of hundred legs and fell from a great height. I was delirious for days.'

Sam went into the kitchen and washed his hands. Brenda handed him the ointment when he returned and she and Gillian watched his enormous fingers as he applied it delicately.

'Are you coming to the farm tomorrow?'

'For lunch.'

'If you come to the smithy I'll put some stuff on to get shut of that poison. I'll give the rest of it a massage while you're there. It won't do it any harm.'

'What about clean vests?' asked Brenda.

He had none, he said. Even this one was not his. He began to put it back on as Sam was preparing to return to whatever he was doing to the church bells.

'No – don't do that,' said Brenda taking it off him and handing it to Gillian. 'Put it to soak. I can get him some more like this one, only not run up. Bob's dad wore 'em. Herself's kept 'em. Keeps everything. I'll not be a minute.' She followed her father out of the cottage.

'She forgot to tell you to keep me warm again.'

'Are you flirting with me now? Would you like some toast?'

'I would, but not yet. It's getting late and I want to take you to the pub to meet Daniel.'

'Tell me, Sir. Why is it that you do not appear to have any clothes of your own?'

'A good question. I made an error of timing shortly before I left the country.'

'And now Miss Marianna Merrivale has all your worldly possessions in her custody?'

'Mrs. Marianna Parker has, or had most of – but not all – my clothes in her custody. She'll probably have sent them to Oxfam by now. They'd be too big, anyway.'

There was no way of telling by his expression what his feelings about this might be. Gillian picked up the vest. 'I'd better do as I'm told. What have I got that won't make you itch?' She went into the kitchen and rummaged about for a bit in the cupboard under the sink.

'Was that a rhetorical question?' came the voice from the other room.

Her next words were going to be: I've been jilted too, you know. But Brenda came in then with five or six well-laundered vests over her arm.

'Will you risk the stepping stones in the dark?' Gillian asked him when he was dressed again and they were taking a short-cut to the King's Head through the back garden.

'Who dares wins,' he muttered.

This struck both his companions as being so funny that they had to lean on the wall at the bottom of the garden for a few minutes to recover. Iain crossed the innocent little brook beyond the wall without mishap and walked across the deserted market square to the door of the King's Head, where he turned and shouted to them: 'Are you stopping there all night?'

'Coming, Sarge,' called back Gillian.

She and Brenda scrambled over the wall and hurried over to him in time to hear, through the open door, Austin's voice shouting for last orders.

SIX

'What's the silly bat wearing jodhpurs for?' muttered Liz, watching through the window as Laura and Daniel got out of the car. Gillian joined her at the sink. It was Tuesday and the first sitting were at the rice pudding stage – in most cases their second helpings.

'Must have decided to squash a ride into her busy schedule for the day.'

'Pity. We haven't got a single horse we could rely on to dump her in the muck.'

'She'll want Columbine.'

Liz brightened. 'She's not been out since Saturday. Slumming again, Laura?' she asked sweetly as Laura stepped into the kitchen out of the pages of Country Life.

Laura inclined her head graciously. 'This,' she said, drawing Daniel forward, 'is Daniel Nesbit. Daniel – my half-sister, Gillian, and Liz Osborne, who is Gillian's cousin.' She made no attempt to introduce him to the seven men at the table, all of whom she knew – indeed two of them, Austin and Brian, were her cousins. But she did award them a group smile and a 'hallo', to which the men responded in their various ways.

Gillian wondered if Laura knew that Daniel had met most, if not all of them, last night at the pub. Probably not, she concluded. And obviously no one had told her either that she, too, had met Daniel last night.

Liz drew Daniel aside and he listened to her with a look of pleased wonder on his unremarkable face, as she asked him solicitously if he had enjoyed his ride here in the Porsche and whether he needed a stiff brandy.

The men were now rising from the table and most of them spoke to Daniel as they passed him. He remembered all their names, Gillian noticed. Laura noticed too. She looked surprised and slightly put out. But she had evidently resolved to be at her charming best today because she schooled her beautiful face into an expression of sparkling interest, which became genuinely animated when the sound of the jeep arriving was heard above the voices in the kitchen.

'I'd like Columbine at one, Liz,' Laura said. 'Just for half an hour. Iain has an appointment with Sam, apparently.'

'Sir!' said Liz, saluting smartly.

'Wrong hand,' said Iain, strolling in.

'Going to get shod, are you?' she asked him.

'Gillian!' said Laura, when they were all seated. 'You don't, repeat – do *not* serve Yorkshire pudding and gravy with fish. Didn't you learn anything at all at that ridiculous finishing school you went to?'

'No, indeed,' said Gillian, in a warm, indulgent voice. 'And you shan't have any if you don't want it. Try some of this nice white stuff here. It's called Gracemire Special White Sauce.'

For some reason, Austin remained behind in the kitchen today. He was propped against the sink and looked as though he was going to stay there for as long as the entertainment continued. His blue eyes, the same blue as Laura's, never left his cousin's face. Laura was aware of this and once or twice returned his regard with a long unsmiling scrutiny. Their likeness was very striking – a very male and a very female variation on the same theme.

The plans for the mill were once again under discussion. Daniel said little throughout the meal, looking delightedly about him through rimless glasses as he ate with visible enjoyment the wholesome perfectly cooked food Gillian placed in front of him, and helped himself liberally from the serving dishes. And yet somehow, without any definable effort on his part, his presence lifted the everyday meal into a successful party.

Laura helped herself to a second piece of Yorkshire pudding, poured gravy over it and embarked upon a graphic and amusing recital of her morning's struggles with Owd Ned at the mill, who remembered her mother and her grandfather and wished to say so at great length, instead of answering her questions about how long it would take to set up the looms for the new orders Daniel had brought.

'Does that mean you'll be taking back more workers?' asked Gillian, bringing another large rice pudding to the table.

'Next week,' confirmed Iain. 'We're sorting out which ones would be the most valuable to get back first.'

'Who likes skin?' asked Liz, spooning creamy rice into a dish and pushing it towards Laura. 'And what about Laura's diversifications? I've had lots more ideas.'

'Let's hear 'em', said Iain. 'I like skin,' he added. Someone pushed a bowl of homemade damson jam in his direction.

'You could turn part of the mill into an educational tourist trap,' said Liz. 'It's old and interesting enough. A working industrial museum – modern looms going hell for leather in the main part and old stuff in the old part.'

'Weaving through the ages,' said Laura, taking fire. 'Someone actually operating a hand-loom…'

'Wearing old-fashioned clothes…'

Everyone was joining in now.

'A shop selling what's been made before their eyes.'

'Tea-room.'

'What about the wheel?' This was Christine's contribution. It led to more ideas and the firecrackers continued until Liz suddenly exclaimed: 'Lord – it's one! Come on Christine.' She ran outside and disappeared; Christine got up and went out too. Laura and Iain finished their coffee then followed Austin out into the yard.

Reg and Daniel were already in the rocking chairs. Gillian stood a moment, watching, to see if the cats would do what she guessed they would. They did: they both leapt up onto Daniel's knees. Nodding to herself, Gillian went over to the sink to deal with the pans.

After a companiable silence, Daniel spoke first: 'Are Laura and Austin twins?'

Reg spluttered into his coffee then began to choke. Gillian ran over to him, removed his cup and yanked up his left arm.

'Mother taught me this,' she told Daniel, as Reg recovered. She went back to her pans, keeping an eye on the goings-on in the stable yard.

'It's funny you should ask that,' said Reg when he could speak again. 'As a matter of fact they were both born on the same day. They're cousins. Mothers were sisters.'

Gillian wondered why Daniel had asked that question. He knew perfectly well that Austin and Laura were not twins; he'd heard the entire ramifications and history of that family last night from the landlady of the pub – Austin's mother.

As she watched through the window, her beautiful Columbine – no longer hers – appeared in the yard, led by Christine, and she forgot about the men behind her. She watched Iain throw Laura up into the saddle and the ensuing spectacle as Columbine pranced magnificently about. Laura somehow managed to keep her seat and look magnificent too. They left the yard at a dashing trot. Gillian closed her eyes. 'You don't trot over cobbles, Laura,' she whispered. She opened her eyes in time to see Iain pulling the forge door aside.

After that something strange took possession of her. She saw her hands turn off the taps; she saw them drying themselves on a tea-towel; she discovered she was walking quickly through the farmyard and into the stable-yard. She felt her body bracing itself to wheel the heavy forge door sideways on its rollers. She had absolutely no right to be doing what she was doing.

Stepping into the forge her automatic pilot switched off abruptly with a jolt of momentary horror as she took in the medieval dungeon scene – the leaping fire, the fearsome instruments on their hooks, the victim facing the wall with his hands braced on the rough stones, the weals on his back livid in the flames, the huge bearded executioner looming over him.

Then the smell of carbolic reached her, the executioner was seen to be wearing a pristine vest and long white apron, the victim was turning around to see who had come in. When they saw who it was they registered her presence as one who was in on things and then turned back to the job in hand. Warmed as much by this acceptance as by the considerable heat that had been building up for the last hour behind that closed door, Gillian went over to the fire and sank down on the giant stool that normally accommodated Sam's bulk.

Sam was already working on Iain's back, using something greenish from an old-fashioned cardboard ointment drum. Gillian saw at once that he was not just smearing it on but was using it more as a lubricant for the careful massage he was applying. She watched the huge fingers as they worked, enthralled by their cunning. Each wound received a special pattern of movement. No one spoke. Sam worked his way down to the poisoned part of Iain's back. It was three inches above his waist – a discoloured patch with an angry puncture mark in it, a curving tail of scar tissue leading away from it.

Sam reached for a second drum, much smaller than the other, and applied a spot if its contents to the puncture mark. He stood a moment, then set to work on the trailing scar where the creature had landed, its poisoned hooks stretched out. Gillian held her breath, marvelling at the gentleness and dexterity of such clumsy looking fingers. At last it was finished. Iain came away from the wall, flexing his back muscles, rotating his shoulder blades and stretching his neck.

'That's better,' he said with unerring brevity. An effusion of gratitude would have been as out of place as an offer of payment. 'We'll have to lock you out tomorrow, Gillian.'

So Sam was going to give him an all over massage tomorrow. Was the enormity of her presence here today as apparent to these two men as it was to her? Ought she to offer some excuse for her intrusion? She had no way of knowing. 'I'm off back to my pans now,' she said, abandoning the question.

They responded with casual farewells. As she slid shut the door she took one last look at them. They were deciding which length of the long workbench to clear for Iain to lie on tomorrow.

She must have been away from the kitchen for half an hour, she realised, when she got back there, because she could see Laura and beautiful, beautiful Columbine charging towards the farm buildings at an unsuitable gallop. Oh well – Columbine's training always went to pot as soon as Laura got up on her. Laura had probably lost control as soon as she turned for home. They would no doubt land safely, however.

Laura came into the kitchen just as Gillian finished sweeping the flagged floor. 'Aren't you going home now?' Laura asked.

Gillian said she was, for an hour or two.

'Good. There's something I want to see you about. In private. I'll not drive you – you'll need your bicycle to get back. Can you be quick? I haven't much time.'

Gillian shrugged, only mildly interested.

As she went for her bicycle she caught sight of Reg and Daniel some distance off. They were standing by a wall opposite the door of one of the milking parlours. Daniel appeared to be struggling with one of the large stones which had been embedded on the top of that wall for several centuries. As she watched, Reg lifted the stone out of Daniel's hands and put it down on the ground. Daniel began to struggle with another, smaller stone. Mystified, Gillian would have liked to investigate. But Laura would be chaffing at the bit, no doubt, and breathing fire if she delayed.

*****

'Ah, you got Laura Ashley wallpaper,' were Laura's first words when she came into Gillian's cottage. 'Or there again – is it Laura Ashley?' She stood for a moment looking around the room. 'You've achieved a good effect,' was the verdict. 'Of course the loot from the Park helps. That clock, for instance, and the grandfather. How did you get it here? Munro, I suppose. Or was it your Uncle Matt & Co.? Why on earth did you drag that piano along? You've surely better things to do now than bang about on that!'

'I couldn't part with it. It used to be in the nursery.'

'I know where it used to be. They tried to get me to learn. Several times.'

And that seemed to be all there was to say about that. Gillian put two small pieces of coal on the fire she had just lit, and a few twigs from the pyramid drying in the hearth. 'When's Dad going?' she asked, wondering what this interview was supposed to be about exactly.

'Tomorrow sometime. He's coming back next week for a few days to finish off at the flats.' Laura was in the kitchen now, pursuing her investigations, even opening cupboards to see what else Gillian had salvaged from their old home.

'Do you want him to go?' Gillian called through to her.

'Not particularly. He's very useful to me in many ways. He's very good at organising. People respond well to him.'

'Parker didn't.'

'Parker's insane. He was probably starting to go mad thirty years ago, or however long ago it was when whatever it was that went wrong between them went wrong in their RAF days. Dad's a perfect host, too, of course, but we knew that. On the other hand, Mother needs him. So he may as well go now. It might not work out to have him still living with me shortly.'

'What might not?'

'About Iain,' Laura said, reappearing suddenly. 'It would be better if you left him alone. I'll deal with him.'

'*Deal* with him?' Gillian looked at her sister in astonishment. 'In what connection?'

'In every connection. It's all going to fit in very nicely, actually. It's time I got married. I'm twenty-seven and I feel one should get the family thing over by thirty-five, so now's the time. Apart from which, I've got several other plans in mind once we've got the mill sorted out – an hotel, for instance. I could be getting that going while I was getting the family thing over with. Falcon Park is ideal. Fortunately he seems amenable. He's given Dad the Rolls, by the way. Once…'

'Just a minute. *Just a minute!* Let my pea-sized brain catch up. He's given Dad the Rolls? Just like that?'

'Yes. And I…'

'You're twenty-seven and want to start a dynasty. I took that bit in. How did he get him to accept it?'

'Compensation for wrongful dismissal. He said his directorship could be reinstated if he wanted. But Dad said no. He's now found his proper métier and doesn't want to turn the clock back. So the Rolls is his golden handshake. Iain made it impossible for him to refuse. So that's settled that. And Falcon Park…'

'…would make a lovely hotel, so you're going to marry Iain to get it. Does he know? I know you're a fast worker but you only met him on Saturday.'

Laura hesitated, but was incapable of uttering an inaccuracy. 'Not yet. But he's obviously out to make amends. The next logical step is to marry me, which will restore Falcon Park to our family.'

'He could do that by legal transfer – or by marrying me,' pointed out Gillian.

'No,' said Laura, with such insulting finality that Gillian nearly threw the bellows she was holding at her. 'No. You wouldn't do at all. Forget it. You'd be absolutely no use to him. He may stay in the army for a few years. You couldn't run his business affairs: I could – and will. And anyway, you're frankly not his type. He's tough. You are far too…unworldly. Inexperienced. Soft, if you like.'

'Thanks.'

'You'd be better concentrating on building up some sort of career for yourself for a year or two. You've made a start, I suppose. I'd have got a lot further myself in your shoes. But you've chosen to start at the bottom and no doubt the experience hasn't harmed you. At least you've started to exert yourself for the first time in your life.'

'I wouldn't say I never exerted myself in the good old days,' said Gillian detachedly. 'Eventing isn't particularly restful. Nor is skiing or skin-diving. Or county tennis. And I did run the Park after…'

'From what I can gather, you've been seeing rather a lot of Iain,' interrupted Laura.

'I've cooked him the odd lunch – yes. But today is Monday and I only saw him for the first time last Friday evening.'

'There's no need to blow smoke all over the room. The point is, you've been seen with him. In church, for instance. I never imagined you'd be so naive as to ask him to go to church with you.'

Gillian let this pass.

'He's mentioned you a few times,' pursued Laura. 'He seems a bit concerned about your way of life; thinks you work too hard – which is absurd, of course. Hard work never killed anyone. But the point is, you must have been telling him some tale of woe for him to think so.' She held up her hand as Gillian tried to get a word in. 'I have to go now. I've to be in Arnside at three. I'll have to change in your bedroom. But first I want to make it clear that that sort of thing is only going to cause embarrassment all round. Apart from which, people are bound to talk if you are seen with him and you'll end up being made to feel a fool when he marries me. People will start pitying you. Or laughing behind your back. Especially after Robin. I'll just go up and get out of these things. I'm going to be late as it is with you interrupting all the time. Incidentally, if you played your cards right, you could probably get Robin back. From what I've heard his firm might be folding soon, so to be connected by marriage to Hampshire Holdings is obviously going to be an attractive proposition.'

This succeeded in depriving Gillian completely of speech. She sat transfixed on the rug, the bellows aimed like a weapon at Laura's departing back. It took several minutes to recover from Laura's Parthian shot.

Slowly she began to build up the fire, giving meticulous attention to the selection and placement of each small piece of coal, twig and wood.

Overhead the ancient boards creaked as Laura moved about. For all her hurry she found time to visit the other bedroom and look through Gillian's clothes. The sound of hangers swishing along the rails came faintly down. When she re-appeared, Laura was wearing a slim navy pinstripe skirt and navy blue sheer silk stockings. The heels of her navy blue shoes brought her height to over six feet. Over the frilled shirt she had already been wearing, she had on a chartreuse blazer belonging to Gillian.

'This'll be miles too big for you now,' she said, briskly. 'I'll buy it off you. It's new. What did it cost? A hundred?'

Gillian shrugged indifferently, wishing she would go.

'It's worth fifty second-hand. I'll bring it tomorrow. I'm off now. Do a few sketches of acorns. You were quite good at that sort of thing if I remember rightly. Design something on that knitting machine I see you've got up there. Anything – so long as it's to do with acorns. And keep away from Iain. What's this?' She tilted Gillian's drawing board forward to see what, if anything, was behind it.

'I thought you had to rush off somewhere,' remarked Gillian dully. She did not particularly care that Laura was about to find out her secret. Quite a few people knew it anyway by now. Her mother knew. And Liz.

Munro knew too, of course. To him she would be eternally grateful as it was he who had, two years ago, found out that she had studied art and design at school, at finishing school and then, part-time, at an art college where she had been the star student of her final year. It was Munro who had chivvied her into the shop in Lancaster, owned by a friend of his from Oxford days; he who had put a stop to her modest protestations and a pencil in her hand; he who had kept her at it, criticized constructively her early efforts; provided unflagging enthusiasm. (Munro, too, had seen the crash coming.)

Finally, it was he who had driven off with the design they were both at last satisfied with. His art shop friend in

Lancaster had a contact in a small but growing wallpaper factory.

When Munro took her second design to Lancaster he brought back with him a present from the firm of six rolls of her first design – a moment Gillian would never forget. Laura was now staring at that same wallpaper, which was now on Gillian's walls.

She was still supporting the heavy drawing board on the arm of a chair with hands shaking with angry excitement.

'Why, *why* didn't you *tell* me? I could have... Who *did* produce it? That on the wall's yours too, isn't it? I can tell by this.' She gave the half-finished work a shake, then carefully propped it so that she could step back to see it from a distance.

'Arnside, Laura. You've to be at Arnside at three, remember? You've got twenty minutes to get there.'

'Look – take that off that board and get another one started. Now! Today! Acorns, oak-leaves, squirrels – whatever you want. But mainly acorns. Get a pillow-slip and measure it first. Right? *Right?*'

'Oh shut up and get out!' shouted Gillian, lapsing suddenly into sisterly rudeness to match Laura's own. 'I'm going back to work. I'll draw you a blasted oak apple tonight.'

SEVEN

By 8 o'clock next morning, Wednesday being her day off, Gillian was at her drawing board, working on the acorn design started late the night before. Shortly after half past nine her left hand removed the busy pencil from her right. The moment had come after which any additions could only detract from the perfect balance achieved. In the early days of her designing, Munro's hand would remove the pencil at this crucial stage. Now she knew herself exactly when to stop.

She took down the board and adjusted the tilt of its table so that she could lean on it to write her fortnightly letter to her mother. Her pen flew across the sheets giving her version of events which, by now, her mother would already have heard about from Elizabeth, her sister, and from Laura, who were both in the habit of ringing her up several times a week.

At the Post Office she bought stamps and was questioned closely about the mill in short telegram sentences by the postmistress. Happy to do her bit towards spreading the word, Gillian discussed the various possibilities with her until another customer arrived – a very old man, who wanted to know what they were nattering about. They told him, taking it in turns to shout in his ear.

He knew all about the waterwheel, he informed them. Worked at mill sixty year, boy and man. Could get th'owd bugger goin' again if that was what they wanted.

The postmistress wrote his name and address on a government form, checking with his pension book to make sure she had the right almshouse, and gave it to Gillian.

The sound of hoofs, just as she reached her front door, made Gillian turn in time to see Columbine's pretty dish-face come round the corner. Then she and Liz were up to her and Liz was dismounting.

'Laura was there,' she said without preamble. 'And Uncle Giles. We had a good time, actually. Keep still!'

'Doing what?' Gillian had forgotten that yesterday was Tuesday and therefore the clay pigeon shoot.

Columbine did not want to keep still so they moved into the lane where she could eat some grass.

'Don't you mess your bit up,' Liz admonished her. 'Where was I? Oh yes. Laura missed everything – she's still a lousy shot – and everyone else hit everything, except Brian. We went around twice and then we went into the pub. And then Laura found that Iain was missing so she stormed off to see where he'd got to. But she soon came back in because he was giving Brian a lesson. The shoot was over and it was nearly dark, but he'd bribed one of the men to keep on firing the discs and he wasn't going to let Brian give up till he'd got at least one, which took him ages, though he did apparently manage three in the end, by which time it was almost completely dark. And Laura was getting madder and madder. You could see she thought it should have been she, not Brian, who was having lessons in the dark. Anyway – Iain and Brian wandered in eventually and she'd no sooner got Iain settled next to her when Uncle Giles…Uncle Giles…'

'Uncle Giles…?'

Your dad came over,' resumed Liz when she could stop laughing. 'He'd been talking to some friends at the bar till then. And he said: are you ready, Darling? I want to get off early tomorrow and I've still some packing to do. And that was that. You know what it's like – once Uncle Giles has spoken, Uncle Giles has spoken! So off she had to go like a good little girl.' Liz paused as Columbine towed her off to another patch of grass. 'The silly ass is so desperate to lasso Iain,' she declared, over Columbine's back, 'she's going to trip her silly self up in her own rope. Can I borrow your bike?'

'Er – yes?'

'You don't mind looking after her for half an hour, do you? Give her a gallop. She'd love one.'

Gillian looked a question.

'I want to see Dad. I've been, but they're making such a row with the wagons and what not. I don't know what the hell they're doing – revving and so on. And the compressor. Columbine didn't like it, so I thought I'd nip here and leave her with you. I was dying to tell you about last night anyway. Just look at that poor dog at the window! Love locked out – or in his case, in. Let him out while you get your bike. He's not seen Columbine for months.'

Jasper shot past Gillian like a bolt from a crossbow when the door was opened and raced across to Columbine. The Arab stiffened and extended a cautious muzzle towards the dog braced in front of her. They sniffed at each other warily. Having identified each other they appeared to be pleased to be reunited.

Gillian soon reappeared with her bicycle. She shooed Jasper back indoors and she and Liz exchanged steeds; she buckled on Liz's helmet, mounted and they rode off side by side, Liz enquiring about the progress of the acorn pattern, which she had heard about at the pub last night.

'And what else did Big Sister have to say?' she asked next. 'She didn't come just to get you to draw an acorn, I'm sure.'

'She didn't realize I could – till she poked her nose round the drawing board. She nearly had a fit. If she'd only known, she said, she could've…'

'And no doubt would've, too. But what *did* she want? Was it about Uncle Giles? Or…'

'I've not got over that yet. What do you think! Iain's given him the Rolls!'

Liz exclaimed suitably about this as she pedalled along, keeping pace with the liver-chestnut's fast walk. 'And that was what she came to tell you about? No keep off the grass warnings, or anything like that?'

'Well – sort of.' As she and Liz had never had secrets from each other she decided she might as well give her the gist of what Laura had had to say yesterday. She did this in a very composed manner – too composed, in Liz's opinion.

She would dearly like to know what feelings lay behind that composure. Typically, she herself made no secret of her own feelings about Laura's plans, which she expressed in appalling language. Gillian listened to all this then pointed out that Liz could not spend her entire life rescuing men from Laura's toils. Had she not done enough, she asked, by snatching Reg from under Laura's nose at the eleventh hour, ruining her education to do so?

But this reminder apparently only served to reinforce Liz's argument. 'There you are, you see,' she said. 'One must make *sacrifices.* These things have to be done on humanitarian grounds.'

Gillian was just about to point out that Liz had decided, at the age of six, that she was going to marry Reg and had never wavered from that decision during the eleven years she had had to wait. But at this point Liz caught sight of her mother in the front garden of her house and promptly swerved across the road to speak to her.

There was indeed a terrible lot of noise coming from the back of the Queen Anne farmhouse where Liz's parents and two of her three brothers lived. The sounds were coming from the concealed area behind the farmhouse where Liz's millionaire father had his scrapyard and her brothers kept and maintained huge earth moving machines, which they hired out, and the lorries they used to transport them.

Columbine winced distastefully as she sidled past. 'I'll bring her back to the farm,' Gillian called to Liz, who was opening the side gate.

'Right,' called back Liz, and disappeared.

'Where shall we go?' she asked Columbine. Columbine did not care so long as it was far away from that terrible noise.

Before the trim frontage was left behind, Gillian pulled up for a word with her mother's twin, who was deadheading late-flowering roses, a gardening apron over her Chanel suit. Gillian told her, in case she did not already know, that today was the day her father was going to Harrogate. Her aunt did know. They speculated for a few moments about how things would turn out, then Gillian said she'd better go before Columbine blew a fuse. Aunt Elizabeth smiled and waved goodbye. It was easy to see where Gillian got her looks from.

Gillian opened the first gate they came to into her uncle's fields. She closed and fastened the gate behind them and off they went, threading their way decorously through Gracemire sheep. Once clear of the sheep she gave Columbine her head. It was not, therefore, her decision (she told herself) that they should find themselves not long afterwards passing the mill at an abandoned gallop.

There were two figures visible near the waterwheel. As neither was Laura, she wheeled her horse around and reined her into a collected trot, rising primly in rhythm as she approached them. She had just remembered that she had an imperative reason for stopping in her jeans pocket.

Sam's indulgent eyes were on her as she said hello, but there was no smile on his companion's face. She looked down at him while Sam moved to Columbine's head. She could read a good deal in those grey eyes before their owner looked away. It did not take a genius to see whose manipulations had now commenced. What on earth had Laura been telling him?

When Iain spoke to her his face, and now his eyes, were expressionless. 'Been far?' he asked. His voice was expressionless too.

'No – it was quite impromptu,' she replied airily. She was not going to let herself make an issue of this sudden change in climate. 'Liz wanted to talk to my Uncle Matt – he's her father – so she went on Columbine. But they've got the compressor going and Columbine didn't like it, so Liz brought her to me. I gave her her head and she brought me here, which was good thinking on her part, because here you are, examining the wheel, and here…' she withdrew the folded obsolete dog licence form from her pocket, 'is the name and address of a very old man who told us at the Post Office this morning that he could get th'owd b…*wheel* going again. If that's what you want.'

Sam took the form and read what was written crosswise on it. 'Simeon Airy,' he mused. 'Must be nearer ninety than eighty. Still has his wits – or had last time I was talking to him. He could save us a lot of time. He'll not have lost the knack. I'll bring him up after he's had his dinner.'

'And you yours,' put in Gillian cheerfully. She could feel Iain's eyes on her but was not going to do more than glance at him for the rest of this interlude. 'Sausages and mash today – Liz's special.'

She smiled unaffectedly at Sam, turned her lovely head to include Iain, and rode off restrainedly, curbing Columbine's wish, which she shared, to fly off at a gallop.

They cantered soberly down to the farm, clearing the intervening hedges, the Arab aware that her rider's thoughts were elsewhere.

So he had taken to heart whatever Laura had been telling him. It was inevitable, really – Laura was nothing if not thorough. In what role had she, Gillian, figured? she wondered. As an ivory tower princess whose affections must not be trifled with? As an innocent village maiden (or idiot) who must not be corrupted by experienced men of the world? As a nincompoop totally unfitted for any part in his life?

Then the likeliest possibility struck her and made her feel quite ill. Yes – that was what Laura would have done: she'd have convinced Iain that she was about to become re-engaged to Robin. Might even have convinced herself as well as Iain that this was so.

When the red mist before her eyes had had time to fade a little, Gillian remembered that she had seen something else in those eyes. And that was strain. Laura was trying to ride him too hard too soon. She was making no allowances for the recent tolls on his strength and health, for the emotional blows that had been awaiting him after his escape.

Obviously his abilities were far above average and it was his own decision to involve himself so soon with the mill, but need he be plagued with whatever extra personal pressures Laura was piling on him on top of all his other headaches just now? Why the rush?

Perhaps Liz was right. Perhaps he ought, on humanitarian grounds, to be rescued from Laura's toils.

Gillian eyed the kitchen door as she was unsaddling Columbine, but decided against it. Liz would be back by now, flying around and glad of help. But no. Iain could arrive at any moment and she was not going to *embarrass* him (as Laura would no doubt put it) by being there when it was known to be her day off. Now was not the time to launch a rescue operation, especially as she had no idea, as yet, how to set about one.

Nor was she voluntarily going to be looked at by him again with his eyes looking the way they were today. She could not quite say what the difference was. She only knew that something was now absent that she had not realised was there. Until it went missing.

Her bicycle was here where Liz had left it. All she had to do was get on it, place her feet on the pedals, and push. She pushed.

*****

'Trouble at Mill,' were Liz's first words when Gillian arrived next morning. 'You look bog-eyed. Where were you last night?'

'Painting Laura's bloody acorns, of course. What trouble at mill?' She switched on a hotplate and put fat in a large frying pan before going off to remove her cherry duffle coat and tie on her cooking apron.

'Daniel's rumbled Bolshie Joe.'

'Oh Lord! And he Laura's cousin. Are they sacking him?' She began to cut off bacon rinds.

Liz was disentangling a pile of sausages and arranging them in the frying pan. 'Not yet. Lunch was like a wake. Laura sat there smouldering and wouldn't speak. Didn't eat much, either. Iain looked fifty.'

Gillian transferred a few rashers of bacon on to the grill pan grid then went back to her de-rinding. What's Joe been doing exactly?'

'Trying to get an unofficial union going ready to hold Hampshire Holdings to ransom the minute the mill starts booming again.'

'Charming!'

'Laura's in a terrible state, torn between wanting to kill him for threatening her ambitions and wanting to protect him because he's family.'

They worked in silence for a few minutes.

'Can you take the ten-thirty out? Christine's got a beginner and I've got to go somewhere.' Liz said this so casually that Gillian paused in the act of placing knives and forks on the table. But no reason seemed to be forthcoming, which was most unlike Liz.

'Who's going?' Gillian asked, laying down the last fork.

'Six of them, but one's Dawn Abbott so you'll have to keep to her speed more or less. The others can dash about with Sergeant Barton.'

*****

Columbine was not pleased at being kept to a restrained trot beside Munchman, when the others eventually cantered ahead after the retired mounted police sergeant; but she had to put up with it. It was Dawn's first time out following a few training sessions with Christine in the field.

They reached the road, turning left after the others and slowing to a walk. Idling along, keeping an eye on Munchman who, as usual, wanted to stop and eat everything green in sight, Gillian became aware of a vehicle approaching from behind. Her ears identified the unique growl of its engine but she forced herself not to turn her head until the jeep was alongside. Then she turned and met the driver's unsmiling look, his brief salute passing too quickly to respond to. She pulled a camel face, forgetting about the large outside mirror until she caught a quick glimpse of his reflected eyes. He had seen that grimace. Oh well.

*****

Laura, Iain and Daniel were late for lunch. Everyone else had started before they came in, unsmiling and preoccupied.

'I'll get it. Sit down,' Laura said, shortly, as Gillian made to get up.

Iain went with her to the range and helped her with the good things being kept warm for them.

Liz, however, had been in a state of covert elation since returning from her mystery trip and was in no mood to allow this lunchtime to relapse into yesterday's gloom. 'How did you enjoy the bingo on Tuesday?' she asked Daniel.

Daniel gave the exaggerated start expected of him but refrained from asking how Liz had found him out. 'Very much,' he responded, with enthusiasm. 'I won a shoehorn. Not an ordinary shoehorn, mind,' he added when everyone except Laura and Iain started laughing. 'It has a very long cane handle and a thong to hang it up by. Did you win anything at that shooting thing?'

'You don't win things on Tuesdays. It's practice only.'

'No need to practise bingo. You should try it.'

But Liz had gone off into some sort of daydream, smiling to herself. Gillian studied Laura's downcast face for a minute then rose and brought a queen of puddings over to the table. She placed a pile of dishes in front of Liz and poked her gently with the serving spoon. Liz came back to earth, took the spoon and dug it into the meringue top of the pudding. Gillian went off into the dairy.

When she reappeared she kept one hand out of sight behind her back. She approached Laura, bowed, then produced with a flourish the document tube she had smuggled in.

Laura leapt to her feet to receive the tube, which she took over to the window, laying it down carefully while she washed her perfectly clean hands. Everyone except Daniel had stopped eating. Liz sat there, round-eyed, the serving spoon suspended. Gillian removed it from her grasp and started to dole out liberal portions. Laura was now gingerly twisting the thick drawing paper out of the tube. There was a long pause as she examined the masterpiece, her hands shaking with excitement. 'Iain – come here,' she said at last.

Liz and Christine went too.

'Wow!' exclaimed Liz after one comprehensive look at it. 'Hurry up and start making them, Iain. I'll have the first four to come off the production line. It's a pillow-slip, isn't it? What about a quilt with frilled valance? I'd like one to go with it. And curtains. And an apron, and…'

'Come and get your pudding,' called Reg who had finished his and was coming over to see what was so exciting on that piece of paper.

Lastly, Daniel went over to the group by the window and it was he, after he had examined it, who rolled it up and put it back into its tube. 'Run me up to the house, will you?' he said to Iain. 'I'll just take this over to Pontefract. We'll get some Falcon cloth over to them for when the technicians have done their thing. They can print there until we get those machines from Macclesfield.'

Everyone was hanging on these mildly uttered words. Without noticing how, Gillian found that Daniel had taken her to one side.

'Duvet covers,' he said in an undertone. 'Single, double, king sized.'

'Have I a king sized sheet of paper, though? And where will I pin it?'

'Sections. You'll think of something. Don't stop up all night again though. You mustn't collapse.'

'She could have a lot of afternoons off,' volunteered Liz, who had overheard.

But Gillian did not want this. They were still arguing when the others left the kitchen.

Outside, Iain murmured something to Laura, who raised her hand in annoyance at herself for forgetting. She came back in and said to Gillian: 'By the way, I've been landed with four tickets for a Sibelius concert tonight. Will you come? You like Sibelius – or did.'

'No thanks. I've got my orders.'

'You have, of course. But you must have worked half the night to get this one finished so you'd better take a break; approach the next one tomorrow when you're fresh.'

Gillian watched Daniel wander away and felt as though a protecting bulwark had been removed. She definitely did not want to be part of a foursome that had the cold stranger in it that Iain had become. Liz, however, thought differently and told her to go.

'You've not been to any music for ages,' she pointed out. 'You'll go mouldy if you do nothing but work night and day. Will Daniel get back in time?' she asked Laura. 'How far's Pontefract?'

Laura paused before she answered. 'It doesn't start until seven thirty. Be ready just before seven, Gillian.' With that she hurried out before Gillian could say anything more.

Gillian and Liz stared at each other.

'And what's come over Big Chief Thundercloud all of a sudden?' asked Liz after a few minutes rumination.

'You've noticed it too.'

'Who does he think he is, looking at you like that!'

'*Not* looking, you mean, don't you? As far as I'm concerned he can suit himself.'

'Have you been quarrelling?'

'Not to my knowledge.'

'It's Laura then. What has she been saying and why is he believing whatever lies she's been telling him?'

'Laura doesn't tell lies. She's too keen on accuracy. She says wild things when she's having one of her mad fits, but she'll not have treated him to one of those yet. Not unless she's slipping. She must be pretty confident that she's succeeded in damning me in his eyes, though, or she'd not have invited me to go out with them tonight. It was only Tuesday she was taking the trouble to warn me off and telling me to stop embarrassing him by throwing myself at his head so much.'

'Puh!'

Liz began to speculate on Laura's possible motives. But Christine soon came in to tell her that her jumping housewives were all up and ready to go.

EIGHT

Brenda was very interested when she appeared in the middle of Gillian's preparations for the outing. She zipped up the very French dress Gillian had thrown on, then found and plugged in the styling brush there was normally no use for these days.

Gillian sat at the kitchen table and reviewed her hands and nails. Not too bad, considering everything. They had suffered terribly when she first started work at the farm and she had lavished upon them all the lotions and potions brought from Falcon Park. She could not afford to buy more when these were all used up but by then Brenda had arrived on the domestic scene. From then on lotions had always been supplied from Sam's kitchen in various containers, some very odd indeed.

She often felt that somewhere, probably in the Bible (in the Book of Proverbs, say), there must be some apt quotation to put in a nutshell the fact that the home-made mixture in the Bovril jar now sitting on her kitchen window sill was as good as, if not better than, the artistically packaged and criminally expensive French concoctions which used to be found on her Chippendale dressing table at Falcon Park.

'Aye – but who's the fourth?' asked Brenda, lifting a lock of Gillian's hair. She twined it around the hot brush and held it for a few seconds.

'Daniel.' Gillian flexed her fingers. There was a roll of drawing paper upstairs which she was itching to bring down. She would much rather be cutting off a length of it, long enough for the top border of a single-sized duvet cover, than be forced to sit still and be groomed for an outing she was not looking forward to, with people she had no urge to look her best for.

'Are you sure?' Brenda stepped back, the better to decide whether to leave the silky waves that framed the flawless face to their own devices.

'What?'

Deciding there was no way of improving on nature at the front, Brenda began to sculpt a pile of shining blonde curls on top of Gillian's head. 'Herself was talking to him at Bingo on Tuesday, like I told you, and he said he'd definitely be at the whist tonight. Could have changed his mind, I suppose.'

Gillian set to work on her nails, shaping them as well as she could. They were very short, but the outcome of her labours was quite creditable when she eventually held one hand out for inspection, the nails oval, pink and polished, the tips whitened in the French way.

'Very nice,' said Brenda perfunctorily. She had nearly finished her ministrations.

Gillian was still looking at her hands. They looked so slim and innocent, the wrists almost childlike. One would never suspect how strong they really were, what work they got through every day.

'If it's that Robin, have nothing to do with him,' said Brenda suddenly, after quite a long silence.

'*What?*' Gillian spun round. The brush, still wound into the last curl, jerked quite painfully.

Brenda unwound the curl carefully. 'There. Doesn't look better particularly. Looked all right to start with. Looks different, though.'

Gillian was staring ahead, outraged, trying to remember Laura's exact words. It was Liz, she recalled, who had assumed, as she had herself, that Daniel was to be the fourth member of the party, and asked how he was going to be back from Pontefract in time. What had Laura said in reply? It doesn't start till half past seven – or some such thing. And now she remembered with great clarity the pause before she said those words. Laura had not lied: she had merely refrained from mentioning that it was not Daniel who was coming with them.

'Yes,' she said slowly. 'That's what she's done. The bitch! And she'll say – even *believe* – that she's doing what's best for everyone. I'm not going!'

'You'll have to go,' said Brenda. 'They're here now by the sound of it. Well someone is. It's not that jeep, though. Anyway – you let everyone know what's what.' Her eyebrows quirked when she saw Gillian's face as she snatched up her white cashmere coat.

Iain let himself in and arrived in time to take the coat off her. She was clutching it so tightly that he had a moment to scent danger before she released it. He held it open for her, exchanging quizzical looks with Brenda, as Gillian thrust her arms in the sleeves, snatched the soft material into place and knotted the belt with a vicious jerk. She looked magnificent.

Iain touched Brenda's curls by way of a goodbye, then followed Gillian as she stalked out, rage flashing off her. He opened the door of the car she was too angry to identify in the gathering dusk. It was the dark blue Granada Estate Munro used to use for marketing and his own purposes in times past. One glance told her that no one else was in it.

She got in quickly, drawing her long, beautiful legs after her, quite a length of them revealed for a split second as she did so.

Framed in the doorway, the soft light behind her, Brenda saw the look on Iain's unguarded face as he shut Gillian in and turned to go round to the driver's side. She nodded wisely to herself, waved and went back into the cottage, closing the door in her no-nonsense way before they drove away.

They travelled in silence until they were almost out of the valley. Keeping his eyes on the road he said, very deadpan: 'Lovely evening.'

'Isn't it,' she snapped back. 'If we're going to Preston we're going the wrong way.'

'It's in Lancaster. I've got directions.'

Another couple of miles passed by.

'Anything happened to upset you?'

'Not yet.'

'Lord – I hope it doesn't then. There's smoke coming out of your ears already.'

She turned her head away. She must calm down and think. Plan. Pretend it was a chess problem.

And when they arrived in the warm and well lit foyer of the concert hall with its bright bar along one wall, there, waiting for them, her inferior knight slightly behind her, was the black-haired queen, in a tightly belted red trench-coat, as magnificent in her different way as her white-queen sister.

Laura's ready words of greeting died when she encountered the unmistakable light of battle in the green eyes confronting her. She recovered herself immediately, however, and drawled: 'Darling – you look positively positive.'

'Yes, Darling,' flashed back the response. 'I'm feeling positively positive. And you, I see, are as ever.' Gillian then turned to Robin, giving him her comprehensive attention.

With the knight's ungainly leap, Robin plunged into speech with a mixture of arrogance, nervousness, patronage and desperation that was painful to watch and hear. She watched and heard.

So he thought she looked fit, did he? Well – she was fit, which was more than she could say about him. Did she want a drink? What a splendid idea. Why not? She said so. Going by the bags under his eyes and a general air of dissipation that hung him he'd been doing plenty of drinking himself in the past few months.

A brandy in her hand, Gillian began to derive a certain savage enjoyment from the situation. A powerful feeling of self-confidence swept through her. Thank Heaven Brenda had had the wit to foresee this. Forewarned was certainly proving to be forearmed.

Laura interposed herself between them, as confident as ever in her own powers to bend and twist people and events to her own ends. Her attention to detail had prompted her to wear (for her) low heels in the interests of not dwarfing Robin too much. But no such considerations had inhibited Gillian's choice of shoes. Her very high heels brought her to the same height as her half-sister, which made Robin the shortest member of the party. Also the messiest, noted Gillian mercilessly.

It was Iain who spoke next, pointing out to Gillian that someone at the far end of the bar was trying to claim her attention. Gillian glanced at the waver, recognising one of her many ex-friends from her carefree and, in this case, show jumping past. She sent her a blinding smile. Presumably the friend was looking so astonished because she, Gillian, was with Iain's party. By now everyone in the foyer had told each other who he was – the national and local Press coverage of his return had been very thorough. And his was certainly the most commanding male presence there.

'It's for charity, of course,' she heard Laura saying. 'That's why all the big bugs are here.' She broke off to assess an antique diamond choker on a passing raddled neck.

Gillian knew that Robin, who had fallen silent, never once took his eyes off her. She could feel them like a weight. She could see him in the mirror behind the bar. He appeared to be mesmerised. He was even forgetting to drink.

Gillian suddenly decided to speak. 'What are they playing?' she asked Laura in a bright, dangerous voice.

'No idea,' replied Laura airily. 'Well – Sibelius obviously. That's why I assumed you'd want to come.'

'And who are playing?' pursued Gillian.

'Yes – well. I haven't a clue. Except they're semi-professionals, or so I read somewhere or other. And there's a brass band or two thrown in for good measure.'

Gillian's laugh suddenly rang out, causing a pause in the surrounding hum. For a few seconds all eyes were on her. Gillian stopped laughing and took an unconcerned sip of brandy.

'The Karalia Suite to start with,' said Iain's calm voice. He'd been studying a poster.

'And Finlandia to finish?' enquired Gillian.

'Naturally. But that's not all. We're to have the last part of his Second, apparently, the Swan of Tuonella and a mystery item which we are invited to identify and write the name of on the form provided in the programme and leave in the box – also provided – at the interval.' The conclusion of this speech coincided with the ringing of the first bell.

At the last minute, sometime after the second warning bell had rung, Laura produced the tickets, handing two to Robin and shepherding Iain away from them. Observing this manoeuvre, Gillian was not surprised to find an aisle and two rows of seats separating the two pairs of seats. Iain handed her a programme as they parted. It had not occurred to Robin to buy her one.

The lights in the auditorium went out, leaving a large assortment of musicians spotlit on the stage. The Karalia Suite soon broke out and swept along with devil-may-care enthusiasm, kept together by the skill of four or five key players rather than by the conductor, a wild looking young man irked by the restraints of the podium he was dancing and lunging about on, but largely ignored by the instrumentalists intending to enjoy themselves to the full. They all finished together too, and the conductor flung himself around to face the audience, flushed with triumph, and bowed deeply several times.

The audience applauded enthusiastically. The evening was going to be a musical success. Gillian relaxed. She had accompanied her mother on many occasions when her sense of duty had dictated that they should support various kinds of amateur performance, and many of them Gillian had endured, almost ill with worry on behalf of the performers. But all was well tonight – in that respect anyway. Her toes were not even feeling the slightest tendency to curl.

But curl they nevertheless did towards the end of the Second Symphony. The players had worked themselves into a sweeping pendulum rhythm that had most of the audience swaying with them and Gillian was having difficulty preventing herself swaying too. It was the fear of touching Robin with her shoulder that was keeping her still and upright.

And then his knee moved inch by inch across to touch hers. With an indrawn hiss of distaste, she altered her position immediately, moving her legs well out of range. A sullen look darkened his face. For a few minutes Gillian forgot the music, her anger against Laura and Robin returning. And Iain? Was he in this too? What did they think she was – a pawn?

When the echoes of the symphony's resounding conclusion had finally died away the orchestra and bands launched themselves into the short mystery item. This was nearly over before Gillian roused herself from her dark thoughts sufficiently to register that the composer of this piece was not Sibelius, which must have fooled many of the would-be winners of the bottle of champagne prize.

A lavish buffet supper had been laid out in the foyer for the patrons' sustenance during the hour-long interval when speeches were to be made. As they walked towards this feast, Robin seized Gillian's arm with almost bullying familiarity. Short of causing an unthinkable scene there was nothing she could do about it. Except freeze.

'Jolly good show, what!' he brayed at the other two as they joined them. 'Liked the first number. You did too, didn't you, darling? I could tell.' He smiled patronisingly at Gillian's averted profile.

Slowly she turned her head to look at him.

'Let – go – of – my – arm.'

'Come on,' interposed Laura hurriedly, taking Robin's other arm. 'Let's get something before these vultures clear the lot.'

Free again, Gillian heard Robin say in an angry undertone to Laura: 'What's going on? I thought you said…'

And Laura's interruption: 'I'll explain later. You can't expect…' The rest of her words were lost in the general din.

Silently Iain handed Gillian a plate. She spared him a quick look. How he must be hating all this. She chose a few random morsels and looked up at him again. He was looking tired. She could have killed Laura, standing there a couple of yards away, heaping her plate and Robin's with smoked salmon and caviar. How *could* she subject Iain to this ordeal? Could she not see how far from fit he still was?

'Did you recognise the mystery item?' Iain asked, after a few mouthfuls.

'Yes,' responded Gillian, still pursuing her own thoughts.

'Want a pen?'

'What? Oh. No thanks. I don't think I'll bother. Did you recognise it?'

'Oddly enough yes. I'm not desperately music-minded but for some reason that piece sometimes gets played in the mess. Someone taped just that bit. Coincidence, really.' He produced a pen and removed the rolled up programme protruding from her pocket. 'A bottle of Veuve Cliquot is not to be sneezed at. You could serve it with faggots and bread pudding, or whatever it is you are going to tempt us with tomorrow.'

She laughed a little at this and wrote her name and the names of the composer and the opera from which the piece came on the form, while he held her plate. He was almost succeeding in defusing the situation.

But not entirely. The speeches over, the prize presented to her, and Iain's soothing presence removed again by several rows of seats and the aisle, Gillian's anger returned. It was now on slow burn. Her companion had wrapped himself in silence, half resentful and half watchful. He made no further attempt to touch her.

The Swan of Tuonella induced a trance-like quality in the well-fed audience; the horn must surely have been a professional. Finally Finlandia, followed by The National Anthem, brought the concert to a ringing end.

Outside, Laura made only a token attempt to persuade everyone to go in search of coffee. Gillian retorted flatly that it was eleven o'clock and she had a full working day ahead of her if no one else had. If necessary, she said, she would commandeer a taxi to take her home if everyone else wanted to prolong the delights of the evening.

Wisely the others agreed to call it a day. Robin bade them a pointed farewell and took himself off on foot. Laura repeated her suggestion of coffee, but only half-heartedly. Iain admitted that he was rather tired and Laura immediately became all warm concern for his welfare, berating herself for not having thought of what a long and tiring day it would turn out to be and urging him to go home and get a good night's rest.

Gillian, agreeing with every word she said, felt a strong urge to kick her.

The journey home did not take long. Gillian refrained from offering to drive and indeed some of his tiredness appeared to have left him. He even made a few tongue-in-cheek remarks to put the heavy undertow of the evening into lighter perspective.

'Yes,' she agreed, playing along, her tone suitably hushed, 'it is a lovely night. What a pretty silvery effect the moon has on those twigs – I mean the lacy tracery of those willowy er…'

'Oaks?' he suggested.

'Oaks,' she agreed.

She fell silent digesting this. Not his words, of course, but his new attitude. It was becoming difficult to keep pace. In this one short week he had progressed from formal stranger to cornered wild beast. He had sought her out, allowed her to see his wounds, been deeply at ease in her company; and she in his. And then turned cold. Yet here he was, deliberately dispensing a light form of banter. Was this the shape of things to come? Was he being *brotherly*? Should she test this theory, she debated, as the car pulled up at her door.

She turned towards him in the near darkness and slowly advanced her lips to his. He seemed to have stopped breathing. Then she changed her mind at the last moment, reaching instead for the door handle.

'Goodnight and thank you for a lovely evening,' she recited.

Roughly he pulled her into his arms. 'Gillian!' His voice sounded menacing. Slowly he let her go. 'Goodnight,' he said. 'I'm glad you enjoyed it. Don't forget your champagne.'

At her front door she turned and raised her hand. He acknowledged her salute as he reversed away from her past the hazards parked along the narrow road. His expression was indiscernible in the darkness, apart from a boding glint in his eye, which made her shiver with something in some ways like fear. But in another way not like fear at all.

NINE

Between them Gillian and Liz unearthed a large pack of faggots from the depths of the freezer.

'Place unopened in pre-heated oven at 450 degrees,' read Gillian.

'Let's chuck 'em straight in the range then. It's going like a blast furnace,' suggested Liz, who should have been elsewhere at this hour of the morning. 'What happened last night? Obviously something did. You're very bright-eyed and bushy tailed this morning.'

'Yes - I am.' Gillian paused in her search for suitable baking sheets, struck by the truth of this. 'I can't think why. It was abysmal in a lot of ways, except that I won a bottle of champagne. It's in my saddlebag. We're having it for lunch. Goes nicely with faggots and bread pud. Or so I've been told.'

'I'm sure it does,' said Liz, pouring boiling water into three large teapots. 'But what *happened*?'

'Well – for a start, Daniel didn't go. Laura had a much better plan up her sleeve. I'll give you three guesses who she trundled along instead.'

But Liz got it in one. 'Not…?'

'In person. The debs' delight himself. Not that he'd delight anyone now unless they were desperate. He's gone off.'

'No glimmer of the old mad magic?'

'Old mad what?'

A satisfied smile swept over Liz's face as she thought of something. 'I'll tell you what it is – you've got her on the run!' she declared. 'It's Laura who's getting desperate.'

It was a thought to conjure with: later perhaps. Meanwhile Gillian stuck to the safer subject of Robin and the sea-change in him. 'Now I've stopped being angry,' she said thoughtfully, 'I can almost feel sorry for him. He is only twenty-six after all.'

She spared a moment to look back briefly over the high spots, or what her naive younger self regarded as high spots, of the eighteen months of their engagement; the racketing about to all the latest in-places with their set of friends. And, to be fair, there was the tennis. They had been very successful doubles partners indeed, she and Robin. There were trophies to prove it, still at Falcon Park: gathering dust, no doubt, like the plans for the for-life partnership which never came off. Yes – tennis had definitely been the best part of the Robin era.

'And looking back,' she went on, 'without the rose-tinted specs., he always was arrogant as well as spoilt by that mother of his. So it must be rotten to be reduced to clutching at straws.'

'I wouldn't describe you as a straw, exactly. Well – not a *last* one, anyway.'

'No, allowed Gillian, cutting lavish wedges out of a whole cheese. 'He certainly seemed struck by the new thin me.' She gave a shudder of distaste, remembering the squashy feel of his knee and arm.

'You *have* taken agin' him!'

'I was a bit surprised myself how totally. *Ugh!*' She shuddered again.

There was no time for more as Sam, Austin and Brian were already filing in. Gillian watched them and the others wolfing down bread and Gracemire cheese and washing it down with tea for a few moments, wondering how bread pudding was made. If soaking was required it was too late. She consulted Eliza Acton and Reg's grandmother's invaluable handwritten recipe notebook. The resulting concoction was very good indeed and several people said so. The champagne, divided scrupulously between everybody, was appreciated also.

At the second sitting, in spite of a brooding tension that hung about Laura, an almost rollicking mood set in.

'What did they play last night, Gillian?' Liz shouted down the table, above the general clatter and talk.

'The Love of Three Oranges,' called back Gillian.

'That's by Stravinsky. I thought you said it was all Sibelius.'

'Prokofiev,' murmured Daniel.

'I *said* Prokofiev,' said Liz. Didn't I say Prokofiev, Reg?'

'No. You said Mussorgsky. Will you please stop shouting.'

'What else did they play, seeing it was all Sibelius?' pursued Liz. 'Tiger Rag?'

'Guess,' said Gillian, serving second helpings of bread and butter pudding.

'Finlandia?' contributed Christine.

'Right first time. They played it last, actually,' said Iain.

'Did you enjoy it, Laura?' asked Liz. She turned to Iain and added in a stage whisper: 'She's tone deaf, you know.'

'She didn't appear to be suffering unduly,' responded Iain neutrally, as Laura did not seem to be listening, being preoccupied with her own problems.

Liz opened her mouth to get in another dig. Reg nudged her in the ribs with his elbow. Liz closed her mouth again and smiled wickedly at Iain.

*****

Cycling home, with strict instructions from Liz not to show her face again that day, Gillian felt so inexplicably euphoric that she had to force herself to refrain from putting her feet up on the handlebars as she coasted downhill where the road dipped deeply into a ravine.

'It's that champagne,' she told herself. Realizing she had spoken out loud she began to giggle. Once started, she found it difficult to stop. 'Shut up, you fool,' she told herself. What on earth was the matter with her anyway? She hadn't felt so giddy since…when?

Had she ever felt like this before, ever? During her engagement to Robin, for instance? If she had it had no place in her memory. She stood on her pedals to cycle up the other side of the dip pondering the question. How exactly did she feel? There was something vaguely familiar about it. She reached the top of the hill and the experience she was trying to recall came back to her: it was that time in the Alps when she and a party of friends had set off on a cross-country skiing expedition. Without warning an avalanche had started somewhere up in the mountains above them.

As she freewheeled down the next hill Gillian felt again the rush of crisp air on her face, the alarm and awe, the mixture of terror and determination to survive, the adrenalin, the confidence they all had in their leader as he led them at terrifying speed, using their skills strength and stamina to their utmost limits to keep themselves – just – ahead of the cascading rocks and snow and, eventually, exhilaratingly, away from the avalanche's path to safety.

Reliving that adventure of four years ago, her speed increased. She hurtled round the next corner and there, immediately in front of her, was a flock of silent sheep. She had to brake so urgently she was nearly pitched over the handlebars.

She could hear Austin laughing somewhere over the wall to the left. One of his dogs was crouched down less than a yard away from her, taking no notice of her, intent on her job.

'It's lucky for you I'm not an avalanche,' she told the sheep at the back of the flock, who were looking superciliously back at her.

'What's that, love?' asked Austin, coming through a gate and closing it behind the last straggler.

'Nothing. I was going too fast. Sorry.'

'No harm done.'

She wobbled along behind the sheep until they reached another open gate, the second dog positioned in the road beyond waiting to head them through it. Austin walked beside her for the few yards. He did not speak. She could feel him looking at her, picking up her vibrations. A very sensitive shepherd, Austin.

She resumed her normal cycling speed and a few moments later was passing the few village shops.

'Good afternoon,' she called out to Austin's mother, who was just coming out of Spar.

'Afternoon,' came the surly response.

Why did that woman not like her?

She promptly forgot Austin's mother. She realized that she was now whistling – in public. Disgraceful!

These giddy high spirits, she told herself, as she turned into Church Row, must be because she had just completed her best design ever. They were because her art had moved onto a higher plane.

They (the high spirits) had absolutely nothing whatsoever, she told Jasper, when she let herself into the cottage, to do with the fact that an oldish looking, battle-scarred man, who you first saw one week ago, happened to look at you today with whatever it was that had been missing for the past day or so back in his eyes.

'And anyway,' she informed the dog, 'he's going away for the weekend to see his mother. And his sister. And his new nephew. So we'll not be seeing him again till Monday. What are you wagging your tail for?'

*****

Brenda took one look about her when she arrived in Gillian's living room many hours later.

'Have you eaten?'

'Eaten?'

Brenda picked up one of the many crumpled balls of paper thrown about the floor and smoothed it out. She looked at it for a moment then collected all the other balls, which she also smoothed out. Gillian watched in owlish silence.

'This one's okay.'

'You're holding it upside down.'

'Chip shop's still open. What do you fancy?'

'Fish is good for the brain, they say. I'll go.'

'We'll both go.'

They took the back way out into the starry night. The crisp air cleared Gillian's brain somewhat. She looked up into the dissolving sky. What a heavenly dark shade of blue it was!

'That Daniel's been getting at Dad. At the whist drive.'

'And?' *Why, oh why, would her new design not come right?*

'Mum's been trying to get him to go public for years of course – thirty at least.'

'Public?'

'His ointments and such.'

Ointment. Iain's back. How was it getting on? Forget Iain for a few minutes. He's been stuck in your head, messing up your concentration, since lunchtime. It won't do.

'Your Laura wants him to tie himself up with the mill some way. I don't see what it's got to do with textiles myself. Diversification, that Daniel calls it.'

'*My* Laura? Bloody Laura! She must be wanting to turn part of the mill into a cottage industry. She'll be getting at Beatrice next. Not to mention Young Sam.'

'Aye – I suppose he could run up some door stops on his forge...'

'Acorn shaped, of course. Seriously though, it is time your father made something out of his cures. They do work – no one can deny that. If they were promoted properly, which they will be if Laura's got anything to do with it, they'll become famous far afield and everyone will benefit: whoever it creates employment for, the general public. Sam too. And Laura will link it to the Bowland Forest range by packaging – those dear little old-fashioned tubs he uses, covered in acorns, say. What about his secret recipes, though? He'll need to patent them first.'

'Your Laura's going to look into that.'

They took their place in the queue. Brenda immediately fell into conversation with two other customers. Moving absently when everyone else moved, a mental pencil started work in Gillian's mind's eye on the lid of one of Sam's round ointment drums. A tiny twirling circle of stems grew. A few microscopic acorns and oak leaves appeared on the stems.

Then the pencil hopped aside and started on something else, entirely of its own volition and not at all related to the decoration of ointment containers. The pencil was quickly called to order and put firmly back to work on a dot of an oak apple. But not quickly enough. There was now a face beside the neat little design, stealing her attention. Doggedly the mind's eye pencil added another tiny leaf to the design.

There – it was done. She would now allow herself to look at that face, that strong, more than handsome face – dark, clever, with longish, thick, slightly curly black hair. But why the beard? The mouth…

'Two fish,' she heard Brenda say.

They brought back the two fish, piping hot in crisp succulent batter. Brenda buttered a lot of bread and made them into sandwiches. After they were all eaten she watched Gillian licking her buttery fingers.

'Did they teach you that at that posh school they sent you to in Switzerland?'

'Of course they did. Liz taught the teachers all her bad habits before she rushed back home to marry Reg.' She picked up a drawing pad and drew a quick sketch of Brenda.

'Mouth's wrong,' commented Brenda when it was finished. She was used to being sketched by Gillian.

They both looked thoughtfully at Iain's handsome mouth on Brenda's pretty face.

'He fancies you, you know.'

Silence.

'Saw him looking at you. You were getting into that car at the time. Last night.'

'Oh Lord! Was I showing all my legs? After all that training how not to at that posh school you were talking about.'

'A bit.'

'Perhaps it's just my legs he fancies.' She raised those long, enviable limbs and propped them on the mantle-shelf.

'There's others fancy you too. Austin does, of course.'

'He fancies everyone.'

'No. Only women. I'm not sure Richard doesn't too.'

'Don't talk daft! He's Liz's brother.'

'He's not your brother.'

Gillian started a full-length caricature of her cousin Richard, known locally as dead-eyed Dick.

'He's not *that* skinny.'

Gillian added a shotgun under Richard's arm, a dart in his hand, a catapult peeping out of a pocket.

Abandoning Richard, she carefully lettered the word FANCY. She began a very pretty border around it. So *that* was all that was wrong with her. She was just *fancying* someone for the first time in her life. What a relief! She could safely let herself look back now and diagnose at what point this strange tropical disease had landed out of the blue and struck her down; could sit back and examine her symptoms and progress; could contemplate being, at some future date, released from its grip.

Deciding that she had probably said enough – if not too much – Brenda changed the subject and began to talk about the Edwardian nightgown and other garments Gillian had sketched one evening and given to her to pass on to her sister, Beatrice, to do as she felt fit with.

'Our Beatie's nearly finished your red nightie. She's putting all that lace on by hand around the neck. This buyer came last week sometime when she was cutting it out. Ordered six when she saw your sketch. And your auntie's booked one of the dresses you drew. Wants it in grey.'

'Which one?' asked Gillian, interested now FANCY was firmly framed.

Her pencil decided to transfer the face, already drawn in her mind, onto paper. This took so little time Brenda's eyes widened. 'The one that'll look nowt on a hanger,' she replied absently, her eyes on the face. 'I fancy him with a beard. Dead macho. Fancy him as he is now though too.'

'Brenda!'

'It's all right – it'll not spoil me for my Bob. It's... What's that word?'

'I can't even begin to guess.'

'Academic.'

Gillian looked at the face. Why had she given him the beard, she wondered? It hid that indentation between his chin and lips that she had taken such a *fancy* to in the mirror at the Grange. Was it as early as that when the symptoms of this novel disorder had first set in? Was that when she felt for the very first time somewhere deep down inside her that odd leap that had kept occurring from time to time ever since, which she had kept telling herself (in her mother's voice) was "just nerves"?

*****

Gillian's heart sank when she saw Laura picking her way cautiously towards her over the cobbles of the busy stableyard. 'You'll have to do,' she told Munchman, whom she was trying to make presentable.

Liz was approaching from another direction with Munchman's saddle.

'His saddle area's more or less all right. I'll do the rest of him by degrees between rides. Hallo, Laura. He's been rolling,' Gillian waved her dandy brush at the clotted mud on Munchman's vast white quarters.

'So I see,' said Laura.

'You're about early, for Saturday,' commented Liz.

'Early? I've done half a day's work. It's nearly ten. Can you spare Gillian for an hour, Liz?'

'Can I?' Liz asked Gillian.

'Depends. The hotpot's ready to sling in at about quarter past eleven. Why? What do you want, Laura?'

'Two things,' said Laura. 'But first things first. We want you to come to the mill and take a look at what they laughingly call the canteen. It's something that needs dealing with but we haven't time to give it proper attention. You've obviously got to grips with catering on a small scale and Iain seems to... To cut a long story short, they've let the old canteen fall into disuse now there are so few of them. They just use one of the old offices...'

'I know that,' interrupted Gillian. 'I did go there occasionally, you know.'

'See you later, then,' put in Liz, helping an eager twelve-year-old up onto Munchman's back. 'I'll see to the hotpot.'

Gillian's eyes followed Liz enviously as she went to mount Columbine.

'So you'll know what I'm talking about. The old canteen...'

'...which is now used as a dump...'

'As a dump – needs putting to rights. It needs stripping and re-equipping ready for when we expand. The ultimate plan is to provide everyone with a good wholesome midday meal like Gillian gives us: Daniel's words.'

'Of course,' said Gillian, drily. 'Never let it be thought that *Iain*, for instance, said them.' She ignored Laura's exasperated hiss at this remark. 'How soon would you expect it to be ready and who's going to run it?' she asked as they walked over to the Porsche.

'In about a month; and someone local. We want local people to do the alterations too.'

Gillian braced herself for the ordeal of riding beside Laura as she waged gladiatorial war with the car's formidable horsepower. Laura put the Porsche into reverse, jolting it backwards at high speed, stopping with a protesting screech within inches of the wall of the farmhouse.

'You mustn't let this job interfere with your designing,' Laura continued as they shot forward. 'All we want is for you to put your mind to it at odd moments during the next day or two – when you're grooming, say – and jot down your ideas, such as what modern cooking equipment would be needed to cater for up to a hundred employees.'

'*A hundred!*' exclaimed Gillian, dazzled by the prospect. It would be a dream come true if so many jobs were going to materialise. The valley's unemployment problem would be wiped out in one stroke.

'At least a hundred,' confirmed Laura, 'if you can keep on producing designs like that first one. Otherwise about fifty. Sixty with the diversifications we have in mind. It's all very approximate of course.'

Gillian felt like clapping her hands over her ears. What if she couldn't produce any more designs of that standard? They rounded a corner, the nearside wheels churning up the grass verge, and screeched to a halt in the nick of time. Sheep again. They appeared to be stationary and with no immediately visible sign of supervision.

'Where the hell's Austin?'

'Not far away,' said Gillian, spotting Blackie, one of the twin cobs, some way ahead grazing loose at the roadside, his reins out of harm's way tucked under the stirrup leathers. She could now also just see Bess, to the side of the flock, lying in wait for her next command. 'Don't do that, you fool!' she snapped as Laura sounded the horn.

'You've altered out of all recognition,' Laura snapped back. 'It's Liz's influence. You're a completely different person.'

'Yes. I am.'

Laura fumed in silence.

Suddenly Bess leapt to her feet. Within seconds the sheep had all vanished through a gate into fresh pastures. The quality of Laura's silence altered for a moment as she shot past the gate. Austin was closing it and their eyes met for a brief second. She did not speak for the remaining few minutes of the journey.

Still rubbed the wrong way by Laura's driving and Laura herself, Gillian stalked ahead into the disused building. 'Is there a measuring tape? She asked irritably. 'And something to write on and with?'

Laura immediately switched on her business persona. 'I'll get them.'

She was soon back with the required items. Between them they took all the measurements Gillian wanted and noted where the power points were and other details. They went outside to inspect the outer walls.

'Silly to waste this view,' remarked Gillian. 'A sheet of glass instead of this blank wall would be lovely. But not practical. We could have a row of biggish windows, reinforced against the gales, though. What about expense?

How much money is Hampshire Holdings prepared to throw around?'

'Hampshire Holdings isn't going to *throw* any money anywhere,' said Laura. The proprietorial note in her voice was not lost of Gillian.

'All right. Whose finger is on the financial pulse? Daniel's?'

She noted the flicker of discontent that appeared momentarily across Laura's beautiful face. Sooner or later, she prophesied, there would be a head-on clash. Or would there? There was no predicting how That Daniel would handle things.

Laura was looking strangely at her. With that penetrating remark and look her playgirl sister had surprised her yet again. Her little sister had been unnerving her all week one way and another – particularly at that concert. Never had Laura found herself less in control of a situation – any situation, never mind one as carefully engineered as that one had been. Suddenly the young half-sister she had taken little notice of over the years, except occasionally as the meek recipient of cordial (if unsought) advice and criticism, had acquired some dangerous weapons, like the powerful contempt she had succeeded in conveying to her and to Robin while outwardly behaving impeccably.

Laura was still smouldering from Robin's insolence when he had finally turned on her as Iain was escorting Gillian up to the rostrum to receive that stupid prize. It had been a mistake, too, to arrange for Iain to drive Gillian to the concert. She had realized that as soon as they arrived and, gallingly, it had been impossible to prevent him driving Gillian home again afterwards.

What had happened during that trip? Iain's attitude had been subtly different yesterday.

The danger that Gillian could filch Iain from under her nose and wreck all her plans must now be taken very seriously indeed. The Robin strategem having failed, drastic measures would have to be taken. Very drastic. Today.

Amid these churning thoughts Gillian's question about financing remained unanswered. She was staring at Laura, a sinking feeling stirring in the pit of her stomach. One of Laura's mad fits was brewing. Gillian could tell by her face, which had become almost ugly. Was it about Daniel's power? Or was it… Now she remembered Laura saying when she first appeared this morning that she had two matters to discuss. No prizes for guessing what item two was going to be about.

In the meantime the sinking feeling in her stomach could go away. She was not in awe of Laura or her mad fits. She was hardly likely to become physically violent and, even if she did, she knew herself to be far fitter and stronger than Laura would ever be. But Laura's driving did terrify her.

'Shall I drive back?' she asked, in a temperate voice. 'I've not driven a Porsche. I'd quite like to see what it's like.' If Laura said no, she'd walk or run back to the farm.

Laura almost hurled the keys at her. She was trying to hang on to her temper long enough to deliver the speech she had prepared earlier and she wanted to deliver it in the seclusion of the car before the chance was lost. If it failed in its purpose, as it now seemed possible, then…

Gillian caught the keys deftly. They were no sooner on their way than Laura drew a deep steadying breath.

'I've had a long talk with Robin,' she began briskly. 'You really are a fool to pass him up. He's quite able in his own line. Iain could easily have found him a niche at Head Office. You could have set yourself up in style in Manchester or Cheshire if you'd only played your cards right.'

'Does Head Office employ many estate agents?' enquired Gillian, her mind on getting the feel of the strange car.

'He could have adapted to some other liaison job or other. He's really quite presentable: wears an acceptable old school tie; speaks…'

'Laura! Did you *look* at him at all the other night?'

'Of course I looked at him.'

'If that's your idea of someone who should be in public relations why don't *you* marry him?'

'Because,' grated Laura, tried nearly beyond all endurance, 'I'm going to marry Iain. I – am – going – to – marry…'

'I hear you. When?'

But Laura could not answer that disquieting little question. Instead she regrouped her forces, tightened her hold on her temper and bulldozed ahead. Since Gillian was hell bent on being criminally unmindful of her own advancement there was obviously nothing else for it but to abandon Robin on life's scrap heap. Had she no conscience about this?

'What's to stop you getting Iain to give him a job anyway if you care so much about him?'

Laura ignored this, frowning at yet another interruption. She, Laura, she ploughed on, would have to be the one to break it to poor Robin that all their joint attempts to bring about happy endings for everyone had met with failure.

'Do you want to borrow my hanky?'

'Don't be so bloody infantile,' snarled Laura, losing control. 'Life's a serious matter. Don't you realise it yet? Will you never grow up?'

There were several things Gillian could have said but did not, giving her attention to her driving. The road was narrow here and winding; the stone walls close.

At the farm they got out. Thankfully Gillian untensed and began to walk towards the stables. But Laura caught her arm. There was a really evil light now in her beautiful Siamese cat eyes. Their slant had become feline: inhuman. Danger came off her in a miasma.

Repelled, Gillian could not break away from her. She had the physical strength to do so but some invisible chain held her in unpleasant thrall.

'I know your game,' came a strangled vestige of Laura's voice. 'You're after Iain. You've been after him from the minute you found out about him. It's a meal ticket you're desperate for. All these paltry jobs you are dabbling in here, they're just rubbish and you know it. Well you're not going to get him, see! Because he's mine. He doesn't want you. Do you hear me? He doesn't fancy you. His sex urge is low. Did you know that? Of course you didn't. You don't know such things exist. They don't exist in that tinpot ivory tower you live in. Such things aren't *nice.* Well I'll tell you something: it doesn't matter because you are simply not attractive that way to men. I can tell. I can always tell. You know what you look like. Your mirror tells you that. But it doesn't *count.* There are some women look like the back of a bus but they get men round them like flies, because they've got an ingredient men can't resist. And you – *you've not got it.*

'Why do you think Robin threw you over when he found out he wasn't going to get all the trappings of Falcon Park?' Laura's voice became shrill and ranting. 'You could never rouse Iain if you took lessons for the rest of your life. You should have grabbed Robin back when you had the chance. He's just about your level. *And Iain thinks so too!'*

Having stared at her half-sister throughout this, mesmerised and not quite believing it was really happening, this final sentence broke through and touched a nerve. With a superhuman effort Gillian stopped herself from fastening her hands around Laura's throat and shaking the life out of her. She tried to speak but no sound came. She wrenched her arm out of Laura's grip. Blind with rage she turned away and ran towards the farmhouse door.

Spent but satisfied, a strange smile distorting her beauty, Laura got back into her car and drove off.

Fighting for control of herself Gillian did not notice Reg and Austin approaching from a different direction.

'My – you look mad,' said Austin coming up beside her. 'I wish you'd get mad like that at me.'

Gillian stopped and looked at him, her teeth clenched. He was smiling at her and Laura's face looked out of his. Her rage boiled up and exploded. He had no time to duck as her flying hand caught his face.

She heard the hiss of his indrawn breath, then Reg's shoulder was between them.

'Will you please stop knocking my men about,' he said mildly, watchfully. He put an arm around her shoulders and led her to the open back door.

Austin followed behind, a hand to his cheek, his eyes bright and intent. 'Not that I'd rather be thumped by you than kissed by anyone else,' he remarked to their retreating backs.

But there was a definite glint in his eyes. Gillian twisted away from Reg's arm and went back to him, defused completely and appalled by her loss of control.

'Austin – I'm sorry. It wasn't you I was hitting. It was just… Anyway – I'm sorry.'

Reg surveyed them both for a moment then shrugged and disappeared through the doorway.

Austin looked down at her as she stared in contrition at the red mark she had made on him.

'How sorry?' he asked silkily.

'Very sorry. Do you not accept my apology?'

'I might.' He studied her face.

Her overcharged emotions demanded an outlet. Suddenly she desperately needed to find something out about herself.

'If?'

'A kiss. No – two kisses. One for practice and one for real.' His deep slow voice was calming her and his words comforting.

But she knew his long-standing intentions towards her. 'You're sure? Only two kisses?'

'More if you want. But that's all I ask: just kisses.'

'Don't you fancy me any more?' This she had to know. It had become very important.

'Yes, love, I do. But I've made up my mind. You shouldn't be handled by a chap like me. But I'll have those two kisses. You hit me, so I'll have 'em. Then I'm calling it a day.'

'That's straight – if it's a promise.'

'I'll shake hands on it.'

Solemnly they shook hands.

'When?' asked Gillian. There was a martial light in her eye. In an ivory tower, was she? It was time she did something about that. Only fit for the likes of Robin, was she? And that only with a financial inducement thrown in? 'When?' she asked again.

'There's no rush. I'll spy out a time when Brenda's out of the way, then come across.'

'Right. Tell Liz I don't want any dinner, will you? Tell her I'm going to finish Munchman off.'

This seemed to amuse Austin. 'I'll tell her', he said, as she wheeled round and marched away. 'Poor beast,' he added.

Munchman thought so, too, when Gillian dragged him inexorably away from the heap of hay in his stall and towed him out into the yard where she tied him by his head-collar rope to one of the iron rings in the wall.

Laura's parting shot flooded her mind as she tackled the horse's filthy flank. No amount of rationalization would make those words go away. It was no good reminding herself that during her mad fits Laura could, and usually did, depart from reality and accuracy; could distort the truth and use it as ammunition. She could stand knowing that Laura evidently considered that she and Robin, even in his present state, were still well matched – Laura could suit herself what she thought. But to think that Iain thought so too made her feel physically ill.

Gillian rested her forehead against Munchman's withers as a wave of sickness engulfed her. In a flash of blinding clarity she knew what it was that she had wilfully been refusing to face up to for days now. She was completely, utterly, passionately and irrevocably in love with Iain Hampshire.

And now that she had admitted it she could not bear it because Laura's words, like cold, black water flung over her, had told her that he had discussed her with Laura and agreed that she and Robin just about deserved each other.

How could he? She must have been fooling herself completely yesterday about that extra quality of warmth she had been certain she could feel reaching her from him.

Blackness engulfed her until she felt that she had sunk into the final pit of bitterness. She remained where she was for a long time, her face pressed into the warm hollow, her body supported against the plump white shoulder. The brush fell from her hand. Munchman rested a hind leg and fell asleep, his steady breathing and his warmth her only comfort.

She did not hear Austin's soft-footed approach and at first it barely registered with her that she was being eased away from her support, so deep was her involvement with tragic discovery.

'There's two sides to every horse,' he whispered, coaxing her over to the mounting block near Munchman's head. Numbly she sat on the lower step with her arm slung over the cold central stone.

Munchman did not mind Austin waking him up, a detached part of Gillian's mind noted dully: Austin had a way with all animals – as well as with women. As the mud began to fly from the steady sweeps of the dandy brush Gillian thought about Austin's notorious powers, which naturally led her on to that other thing, niggling like a trapped nerve. An ingredient, Laura had called it. And she, Gillian, had not got it, whatever it was, that could light Iain's inner fires. Or, Laura had also implied, anyone else's either. Laura, presumably, had that ingredient. Had *she* succeeded in lighting Iain's fires?

When she could not stand thinking about that any more she watched Austin walk around Munchman to finish off the side she had abandoned, and thought about her pact with him instead.

One thing was certain – Austin was known to be so highly flammable that if she did fail to ignite him she would know for sure that Laura was right – about her lack of that magical power if nothing else.

TEN

Austin had to wait until Monday evening for his kisses but he was quite philosophical about this. After all, he had been waiting for seven years at least; another couple of days wouldn't kill him.

What he was rueful about was the timing. If only this had cropped up four or five months ago – sometime after Easter, say – when, suddenly stripped of her Daughter of the Manor status, Gillian became overnight an attainable object. And not only no longer remote and above his reach but, incredibly, taken on at the farm! In constant contact with him; actually attending to his daily needs. (Well – some of them.)

If only this had cropped up sometime after then but before that chap landed from outer space and altered everything. And before he, Austin, had made a certain decision on that other matter.

But that decision had been made and that chap had landed; was still altering things; would no doubt go on altering many more things – and lives – before he'd done. And good luck to him. And goodbye Gillian. He'd faced up to that. A cook/groom Gillian might be just now but it'd be daft not to see she was still destined for that chap, or the likes of him, not the village shepherd/stud. He could never have married her anyway – not with things being as they were between the families. But she'd have been his star conquest if only he'd had his way in time: the ultimate…

Still and all, she'd caught him a hefty wallop back there and his face was still tender. He'd have gone down if he'd been off-balance. (Must be all that tennis she used to play.) So he was going to collect. Pity he'd already made up his mind and so had settled for just kisses. But there it was.

And another thing: he didn't like to see her upset like that. He'd got very fond (as well as the other thing) of her these last months. Plus he'd a score of his own to settle with dear Cousin Laura. Could be he could do Gillian a good turn while he was at it. He'd have to get his skates on, seemingly. Meanwhile…

*****

Meanwhile, Gillian spent Sunday not getting on with the duvet border. The drawing board was up and she spent several hours seated before it and occasionally her pencil became busy. But six o'clock came and went and all that was to be seen on the long strip of paper pinned up there were four or five forlorn acorns and a misshapen oakapple.

At that point she noticed the time, flung the grotesque caricatures she had done of Laura into the fire, together with her dreams and, decisions made, went to church with iron resolution in her soul.

*****

On Monday morning she received without any change of expression the news that the mill contingent would not be dining at the farm today because Daniel had called a meeting at Falcon Park of the higher management of Hampshire Holdings. They would all, Liz reported, be having a buffet lunch at The Grange.

Gillian merely shrugged. If Liz expected her to wail and gnash her teeth at being deprived of the sight of Iain, or Daniel, or Laura – especially Laura – she was, she said, sorry to disappoint her.

'I gathered there's been a rift in the lute,' replied Liz temperately. 'Why did you go and beat Austin up though?'

'It wasn't actually Austin I was beating up when I beat him up.'

'Oh – I see.' Liz saw.

'Anyway, I haven't time to stand here chattering about trivialities. I've a canteen to plan.'

And a few more layers of steel to add to her new armour.

The day crawled by and evening came. Austin took up his position near the front windows of his parents' pub where he could keep watch on the rear windows of Gillian's cottage. From time to time he caught glimpses of Brenda as she went about her self-imposed tasks. Then the lights went out and when he saw her next she was within feet of him as she passed by his window on her way to her parents' home. He was counting on this: as the whole village knew, today was Brenda's mother Alice's birthday.

Austin strolled outside and looked up and down the street. It was nearly dark. Almost immediately he saw Gillian's bicycle lamp proceeding across the end of Market Street along the main road. As he looked, the beam wavered and the bicycle stopped. A puncture?

He strode over to her. A few moments later, those out and about at that time noted that Austin seemed to be doing a genuine rescue of a maiden in distress for a change.

'Soon have this mended,' he said cheerfully. 'Got a kit at home?' He turned the bicycle upside down and slung it over one shoulder.

'Thank you. Yes, I've got one. Two actually. Can you manage?' This in her best Lady of the Manor voice.

'Course. Weighs nowt,' came the stout reply.

This pantomime concluded they set off for the cottage, a decorous distance between them, determination hidden in both hearts: his to make the utmost use of his two kisses; hers to do something drastic about smashing down walls of ivory towers.

Jasper made a tremendous to-do on their arrival. He knew Austin well, of course: Austin knew every dog and every other animal in the valley. But he had never been here before and Jasper proceeded to mention this at the top of his voice. Austin flicked the bicycle back onto its perfectly sound wheels and followed Gillian with it through the passage between the cottages to the shed in the back garden where it and coal were kept.

'Don't turn on the light,' he said quickly as she led the way through the back door, seeing her hand go automatically to the switch. Gillian hurriedly withdrew her hand.

'Whoops! What about the fire? Brenda must just have lit it. It's not up to much yet.'

'Lie down,' he said to the dog, who was now wearing his teacher's pet look. Jasper lay down.

There were no more words. Austin moved quickly to where she stood outlined dimly, taking off his jacket. His arms went firmly around her, tightening as he moulded her slim body as close to his as he possibly could without hurting her. His male smell came to her with a faint tinge of beer on his breath as his mouth found hers. She took a deep breath, closed her eyes and yielded, putting her arms around him.

He was certainly an expert. It was amazing what his lips could do without once leaving her mouth. This was Kiss One and he intended it to last a long time. Kiss Two was going to be different.

As though it were not happening to her but to someone else, she noticed that his notorious animal pull was beginning to have its effect. A novel kind of warm weakness crept slowly over her. Austin released her.

'Right love,' he said cheerfully. 'Now for the real thing.' He began to remove his shirt.

Gillian watched him in the glow from the fire, grown brighter during their first kiss. How unlike Laura he looked now his colouring was not distinguishable. His outline was all male. Also the hairs dimly visible on his chest. How strange it was, she thought, that after five months of chaste female comings and goings this demure little room should be entertaining its second half-naked male within one week!

Austin's hand was reaching tentatively towards the buttons of the high-necked shirt she was wearing. She laid a restraining hand on his and he desisted immediately. It was worth a try, said his cheerful shrug.

He turned her slightly so that the young flames lit her up. 'Lovely. You're lovely. Lovely.'

'Austin – you sound just like your Brian!'

'You *what?*'

'When I let him have Nescafe in his hot milk.'

He laughed unsteadily and drew her against him, savouring her beautiful contours before taking his final kiss. He evidently had no qualms about letting his work-roughened hands rasp her soft skin. Nor did she dislike the feel of them.

So *there*, Iain Hampshire! she thought defiantly. So much for you and your vows not to touch me until… But she was not going to think about Iain Hampshire. He would never touch her now, so what he was going to do with his hands when and if they were no longer rough was of not even academic interest to her. What was of *real* interest to her, she told herself, was what she was experiencing here and now with this quite different man and, more importantly, what he was experiencing with her.

Her fingers curled among the black hairs on his chest. When he bent to take his kiss her lips were ready for him. He kept his promise. Almost she spoke when at last he released her. But something stopped her from saying the words that would keep him with her longer, allow him to continue.

And true to his word he did not kiss her again. 'No,' he said. 'I must leave it at that. It's not fair to go any further. Not fair on either of us.'

He paused in the act of putting on his shirt. She stared up into his handsome face, revealed by the strengthening flames. His words, when they came, were the very ones she needed to hear, were balm to her bruised soul.

'There's not one in a thousand would – could – leave it at that,' was all he needed to say, the so close allure of her beautiful face in the firelight making his voice even slower and very deep. 'But when you clout me again…'

She smiled her first smile since Saturday and pulled his head down to lay her cheek against the one she had struck. 'When I clout you again…?'

'If you're going to, you'd better make it soon.'

'Why, Austin? Are you leaving the country?'

'No. But I'm twenty seven. Time I got married.'

'You and Laura both.'

'*Laura?*'

'So she said.'

He was silenced, but Gillian hardly noticed. She moved away from him and prowled thoughtfully about for a few moments, still in need of more reassurance.

'Would you like to be married to me, Austin?' she asked. 'I'm not proposing,' she added hurriedly, knowing that what she had just said sounded exactly as if she were. 'What I mean is, do you think the average man would consider having me as a wife?'

He took his time answering, tucking his shirt into his trousers. 'Someday, love, you're going to make the right man very very happy. But he won't be just average. He won't be me, either.'

'Oh.' She would have liked to ask why.

'My mother doesn't like you for one thing.'

'I gathered that. But why?'

'Nothing personal. It's just that she wasn't suited when your father married your mother so soon after Jess died, being her sister, see?'

She saw. The fatal family bitter streak.

'And she doesn't like you giving Brian all that milk,' he added after a thoughtful pause.

She giggled involuntarily at this very odd news. 'Why ever not?' she asked faintly. 'He needs all the building up he can get, shooting up like that.'

'She knows that and she wants to build him up too. But he won't drink milk for her.'

'Really?' For a second or two she felt quite touched that a six feet five inch tall teenager would drink milk only for her. Then her mind went back to something elusive trying to claim her attention. That was it: the quality of his silence after she had mentioned Laura. Another matching memory clicked into place a moment later – the quality of Laura's silence as they drove past Austin on that nightmare trip to the mill. And, she remembered next, there was Reg's reaction when Daniel asked him if Laura and Austin were twins, knowing full well that they were not. Reg choking, she now realised, would have confirmed an idea Daniel had got hold of from somewhere – probably, knowing Daniel, plucked out of the air.

Without stopping to think or choose her words, out came the question: 'Austin, have you ever made love to Laura?'

Her words stopped his movements in the middle of putting his jacket back on. He did not answer straight away.

'It's one of my rules,' he said at last. 'I don't tell. I'll not tell anyone I kissed you tonight and don't you go telling anyone either. It won't do you a mite of good. Might do you some harm. So keep it a secret between you and me. Right?'

She stepped closer to him and put her arms loosely around his neck. 'I'll promise I'll never tell anyone if you tell me whether you've ever made love to Laura.'

Her nearness was affecting him. He put his hands in his pockets. She tried to shake him, but not very hard, and he stood like a rock, his tanned face thoughtful.

'Tell me,' she whispered. She had to know.

'She was my first.' His voice, when he at last spoke, was deep and quiet in the stillness. 'And I was hers.'

Gillian kept perfectly still, her arms on his shoulders.

'We were sixteen. She found out everything she wanted to know. And so did I. Then she chucked me aside like an old sock. And…' His voice, turned suddenly ominous, stopped.

'And what, Austin?'

'That's the other matter I'm going to settle before I get married. And you'll keep that to yourself too. Or I'll… I'm off now.'

His mind was obviously made up so she gave him one of her warm friendly kisses, which he returned in the same spirit. Then he left her, not allowing himself a backward glance as he let himself out of the back door.

'Well!' she exclaimed, subsiding with a bump onto the saddle stool.

A tongue of flame broke through the logs, followed by three others. The fire was taking hold properly now and suddenly the room was brightly illumined. Jasper sidled close.

They both gazed into the fire for a long time. Rousing herself when the flames began to falter and subside, she built up the fire with logs and coal. The blank blackness of the window caught her eye. She moved over to it to look out into the night. Faint sounds reached her from Alice's party at the pub. She drew the thickly lined print curtains together with a clash of brass rings, loud in the quiet room. Still she did not put on the light. The fire would soon brighten the shadows.

The longcase clock chimed the half and then the hour. Subconsciously she started counting as the strokes of nine o'clock boomed out. The clock was still striking when there came a sharp double-rap on the door.

Gillian jumped violently, a split second before Jasper, roused from sleep, leapt barking at the door. He stopped to sniff loudly at its bottom edge. Having identified the visitor he waited eagerly for his mistress to open the door.

His mistress, however, was paralysed with a welter of emotions. She knew with complete certainty who was out there. That double-knock would be sounding through the chambers of her heart forever. Why did he not barge in? He usually did. Usually? Usually? He'd only been in her life five minutes – not a lifetime! She had been through so much since last she saw him she could not for the life of her remember on what terms they last parted. Frantically she clawed together the rags of her wits.

For a few moments after she opened the door no words were spoken. She stood framed in the doorway, the fire lighting her dramatically, contemplating his unsmiling face.

'I see the novelty of barging into people's homes without knocking has worn off, Major Hampshire.' Her voice sounded brittle and hostile.

'After dark – yes.'

She remained where she was, barring his way.

'I'm coming in, Gillian.'

'Not if I say not. You have no seigniorial rights here, Major!'

What on earth made her come out with such a damn silly word with all its implications, she asked herself. And in reply could hear a host of invisible Freudians sniggering at her. She was furious with herself, and now, not reasonably, with him too.

His forearm came up at shoulder level. There was no suggestion of violence but there was nothing she could do about it. She stood her ground as strongly as she could, gripping the doorposts, but it was only moments before the inexorable pressure forced her back.

Once in he turned to close the door.

'You have a chain on this door, Gillian. You should use it – after dark at least. Anyone could come in. With or without seigniorial rights.'

He moved towards her, avoiding the central lamp he was too tall to stand beneath. She reached out for the light switch. His voice, quiet but menacing, made her pause.

'There's no need for extra light. I can manage just as well by firelight.'

She switched on the light, her eyes glinting dangerously at him. 'To do what, exactly?'

'Nothing drastic. Jasper here will have no cause to intervene this time. Why don't you sit down? Here in this armchair will do. You could put up your feet, even. Close your eyes. I'm sure you must be tired.'

Her anger subsided as she examined his mood. She remembered now – they had parted perfectly amicably on… Friday, was it?…the missing spark back in place every time he caught her eye. And now here he was, storming her citadel, speaking solicitous words in a tone that she couldn't quite fathom but was certainly not solicitous. Was he looking for a fight?

'Of course I'm tired,' she said with spirit. But she had no intention of sitting down while he was stalking about like this. Instead she waited to see what he would do, or say, next.

What he did, took her so completely by surprise that for several seconds she was paralysed again, which gave his scarred and ill-used fingers time to pluck delicately at the top button of her blouse until it was eased through its buttonhole.

Then animation was restored to her. For an instant a treacherous demon tempted her. She dealt it a sledgehammer blow. Her hands flew up.

His, however, were even quicker and out of reach before she could tear them away from her.

'If you hit me,' he said, anticipating her next move, 'I'll know that you want me to hit you back. Here – hold this a minute.'

He withdrew a small object from his pocket and held it out to her.

Slowly she lowered her eyes to blink in disbelief. It was one of Sam's familiar ointment drums, smaller than any others she had seen, being less than an inch in height and diameter. On its lid was scribbled the word BRUISES. Its significance was immediately clear to her. As she had uncovered his wounds last week, here in this room, and caused them to be ministered to, he was now proposing to do the same thing for her in return.

'Will you sit down now?'

'No,' she answered as she reached out and took the ointment from him.

'I didn't come here with the intention of sweeping you off your feet,' he stated conversationally, sweeping her off her feet before she could guess his intention.

Excitement rose in her as she felt his strength, before he dropped her, none too gently, in the armchair. Her feet were raised up and placed on the wall beside the fireplace, on the spot where feet had obviously rested many times before.

Gillian closed her eyes. She was back in the Alps, going down and down and down.

Relapsing suddenly to her schooldays she muttered a string of Old English oaths under her breath. 'Damn,' she added for good measure, as she waited for her breathing to return to normal. And for inspiration to come. At all costs she must not let him know… Not let him see… He was the man who had decreed Robin a suitable mate for her, she reminded herself urgently. The man she would probably have to have as a brother-in-law for the rest of her days. The prospect steadied her.

She took a deep breath. What she must now do, and quickly, was put on the armour of a light and flippant attitude to shield herself from herself. If she was doomed to be his sister-in-law she might as well start rehearsing for the part now – this minute. One more deep breath.

She half opened her eyes to peep mischievously at him. He had the next two buttons undone by now. She raised her head so that he could fold back the ornate high neckband of her blouse to reveal the yellow, still itchy marks left on her throat by his murderous fingers.

'What about your vow not to touch me?'

'I haven't – yet – with my hands. I went to some trouble back there not to. You evidently didn't notice.'

'What makes you think I don't like the feel of hands that are roughened by honest toil? And anyway, how are you proposing to transfer that ointment onto my bruises without touching me with your fingers?'

For an answer to her second question he produced a small polythene bag containing a few cotton-wool balls.

'I don't like the idea of my hands in their present state touching female flesh.'

'No wonder Laura was grumbling,' she muttered, as if to herself.

'What exactly was Laura grumbling about?'

'Your low…profile.'

He drew up the saddle stool and lowered himself on to it. He was now very close indeed. She could feel his warm breath on her face. The fire had reached monumental proportions, making the flickering glinting room very warm indeed. With a quick movement he ripped off the thick Aran sweater he was wearing and tossed it to the back of the room. She turned to look at it where it had landed on the sofa.

'Where on earth did you dig that up from? My mother knitted it. It must be at least fifteen years old.'

'Mrs. Appleton produced it. Do you like the feel of toil-roughened hands?'

'I wonder if she found it in the boiler-house? Dad could never bear to throw away things we'd knitted for him so he used to lag pipes with them when they got too old to wear.'

'You haven't answered my question.'

'Mmm,' she muttered as she closed her eyes. He was at liberty to choose whether this murmur of contentment was prompted by the thought of work-roughened hands touching her or by the soothing quality of the cream he was applying to her throat.

His task finished, he remained where he was, his arms resting on the arm of her chair. After a while she could not resist opening her eyes to look at him. There was still no glimmer of friendliness in his eyes. But they were not as cold and bleak as she knew they could be. They were sort of watchful, she decided. He'd got the bruise tending – the debt settling – over with; and now there was something else. If he started to lecture her about Robin she'd probably throw something at him.

'Why was Austin here tonight?'

The words hung in the air between them. She closed her eyes again. It was easier to think when she could not see those clever grey eyes so close to hers. So he was coming the heavy brother-in-law already, was he?

'How well informed you are.'

'Not always. I now know that I was misinformed about your present relationship with Robin. But my own eyes informed me that Austin climbed over your back wall about an hour ago.'

'And this interests you?' So he hadn't come to plead Robin's cause. It was her morals generally he'd come to investigate. In his role of Big Brother, no doubt.

'Are you involved with him?'

'Of course I am. I cook his breakfast more often than not. And his lunch. I feed his dogs.'

'It was not breakfast or lunchtime an hour ago and his dogs were not with him. What exactly took place when he was here?'

She sat up suddenly, lowering her feet and opening her eyes.

'What we obviously were *not* doing,' she said, 'was making wild, passionate love. We can't have been because...' she lowered her voice confidentially, 'I've got an ingredient missing. You'll have noticed that for yourself. That's the real reason why you don't want to touch me with your hands.'

'Word games, Gillian.'

'Pass me that tin, would you please. I'm falling behind with my work what with one thing and another. The canteen...'

'What were you and Austin doing?' he interrupted, implacably.

'All right – I'll tell you. Why, I don't know. Do I cross-examine you? I owed him an apology.'

'For what?'

'For hitting him. Would you like to switch on that lamp so that you can shine it in my face? I believe that's what they do when they're interrogating prisoners.'

'You had a good reason for hitting him?'

'No reason at all. It was a total mistake. I was a bit upset at the time about something and his face happened to get in the way of my hand. By accident.'

'What had upset you so much that you were lashing out?'

'That, Major Hampshire, I am not going to tell you.'

'What form did this apology take if he had to come here to collect? You kissed him, I suppose.'

Gillian appeared to give this question a great deal of thought, ignoring his tone. 'Yes and no,' she pronounced at last. After all – she had not actually given Austin her word that she would not tell anyone that he had kissed her. 'It was more sort of pre-arranged and mutual. Wait a minute, though! Yes – I remember now: I did kiss him, just as he was going. But that wasn't apologising for anything – more a sort of thank-you for something else.'

She looked with interest at his clenched hands, their knuckles white with the restraint he was keeping on them.

'What else would you like to hear about?' she enquired. 'Or is it just kissing you're interested in?'

'By all means tell me who else you've been kissing.'

'Let's see now. Where to begin? A week last Friday's probably the best place. Before that, months and months went by kisslessly. Ever since Robin ditched me, in fact. Did you know that Robin jilted me? You see – you're not the only jilted person around here. In my case I wasn't ditched because I vanished but because Falcon Park, et cetera, vanished. Where was I?'

'A week last Friday.'

'That was Terry. He kissed me once or twice outside that very door. It was quite pleasant. He smelt nice. Good dancer, too. I was in shock of course.'

She waited a moment to see if he would comment on this last remark. He did not, but it was plain from his expression that he had divined that coming face to face with him, in that mirror at the Grange, was the shock she was professing to.

'And that's it,' she concluded. 'Austin kissed me tonight. Twice, actually.'

If only that silly voice in her head would shut up, instead of whispering, coaxing, tempting. Of course she wanted to kiss him. But she was *not going to!* she hissed back at it. She – would – not – look – at – his – mouth. 'And there was one other,' she heard herself saying. 'But we won't go into that.'

'Do go on,' he invited, drily.

Okay – you win, she sighed to the volley of suggestions and exhortations buzzing round in her head. She smiled and summoned up all her theatrical forces.

'It was Sunday,' she began in a low dramatic voice. 'Very early. My dog and I were rushing about harmlessly, enjoying the newly minted day. Suddenly,' her voice rose, thrillingly, 'a wicked lord leapt out at me from behind a tree where he was lurking with intent to sweep me off into his castle. He captured me! He cooked me a huge and utterly delicious breakfast. Which we ate.

'And then…' her voice sank dramatically, 'he collapsed! What was I to do? We struggled through into what he appeared to think was the right bedroom and I laid him down to rest. He slept. Or so I thought. Suddenly, he grabbed my head! Like this. I thought my last hour had come…'

The frown of pain on his face stopped her. She was not gripping his head tightly enough to hurt him, so it must have been her words, her reminder of when her last hour nearly *had* come at his hands that was causing him pain.

'And then,' she went on, huskily, 'he said: get lost, Mother, or something like that. And he kissed me. Like this…' She left a butterfly kiss on his lips then drew away from him. 'Well – like that only more so,' she amended unsteadily. 'Obviously he's better at that sort of thing than I, being a bit older. How…?' She broke off and gazed wonderingly at his transformed face.

'I'm thirty, Miss Falconer,' he said softly.

He leaned forward slowly until his lips were on hers.

*****

She lay in her chair listening to the activities in the kitchen; heard him fill the kettle and switch it on; heard the spoon in the tea caddy rattle, the bread bin lid open and close, the butter dish lid lifted and replaced.

He brought in the bread-board which he placed on the saddle stool beside her. The toasting fork was lifted from its hook on the wall and put into her hand, the first slice of bread impaled upon it. Tea arrived in coffee mugs with milk but no sugar. It tasted like nectar to Gillian, who normally took sugar.

Now he was lounging on the hearthrug near her, having relieved her of the toasting fork. They shared the first slice of toast between them.

While he was toasting the fifth or sixth slice a pile of sketches caught his eye. He drew them closer and began leafing through them. Some of them were the ones Brenda had rescued and uncrumpled the other night.

'This one's good – apart from the poor squirrel. It's upside down.'

'It's the rest of the picture that's upside down, not the squirrel. I'm probably going mad.'

'Mad *and* an ingredient short? What, by the way, is the nature of this ingredient, mysteriously thought to be missing? It's not physical, I'm sure. Is it mental? Spiritual?' He continued to turn over the sketches.

'It's difficult to define,' said Gillian. 'Chemical, perhaps. Or magical. That toast's burning.'

'You like beards?'

'Why? Oh – I see. I thought I'd burnt that one.'

'Symbolically?'

She did not reply to that.

'I ought to be at the pub,' she remembered drowsily, sinking lower in her chair. 'It's Alice's birthday.'

'There's plenty of time. You're not going anywhere like that.' He nodded at the open neck of her shirt.

'Heavens – no! Austin might want to know exactly what you and I have been doing, shut away in here all this time.' She began to put things to rights.

'Allow me,' he said, hurling the burnt piece of toast in the fire.

She concentrated carefully, hoping to feel his fingers on her skin so that she could point the fact out gleefully to him. But he was too dextrous and within seconds the three buttons were fastened, her marked neck concealed again.

'You let Brenda hold your hand,' she remarked as they went down the garden. 'And she's younger than I.'

'I let Brenda *examine* my hand. You told me Brenda was a nurse.'

'She was a nurse,' allowed Gillian, 'until she married Bob. She's a hairdresser now.'

'Can she trim beards?'

Across the cobbled square the door of the pub swung open letting out the sound of Austin's joyous baritone singing '*There's a hole in my bucket…*'

'He is in good voice,' commented Iain drily, lifting her neatly over the wall.

'Ssh!' She held up a finger as Austin stopped singing and contralto exhortations came floating out of the pub to '*mend it, dear Henry, dear Henry, dear Henry.*' 'That's not Alice.'

'No?'

'It's Brenda. She must be drunk. She never sings when she isn't. Pity really. Her voice is nearly as good as Alice's, even if she can't smash glasses with it like Alice can.'

Daniel came out of the pub as they approached. 'There you are,' he remarked mildly. 'I'm off home now.'

'Got any more names?'

'Hundreds.'

'Hang on. I'm for my bed too. I'll just see Gillian safely into this orgy she's supposed to be attending.'

He settled her on a high stool between Sam and Brenda (Brenda having procured the stool for her by the simple expedient, in mid-verse, of pushing one of her brothers off it) and asked her what she wanted to drink. Sam took charge, pointing out that there were more than enough drinks lined up already.

Having assured himself that she was in the safest possible hands Iain departed after brief farewells all round. Gillian let out a long breath and reached for the nearest balloon glass.

ELEVEN

The frisson that caught her when Iain's tall figure emerged from the driving seat next morning was so fierce that Gillian had to put down the jug of gravy she had just made and clutch the sink for support. So much for her overnight resolve not to let herself read too much into last night's events.

Through the window she saw him move around to Laura's door and open it. Laura, predictably, made a mega-star production of getting herself out of the low and awkward seat, holding out her hand – *which he took!* A welter of uncivilized emotions caught Gillian such a body blow she almost fainted.

And she had been so certain that she could remain cool and detached; could wait and watch. She watched them cross the yard, Laura's arm tucked under Iain's, her handsome face tipped up to him in earnest discussion.

The men were coming into the kitchen. Accustomed to dealing with troubled daughters, Sam collected her automatically on his way past. Unresisting, she allowed herself to be steered over to the table, the gravy left forgotten by the window. Like an automaton she transferred brimming bowls, two by two, to the waiting men and to Laura. She somehow managed to conceal her upset; managed to appear to be her usual untroubled self.

She did not notice that Austin was not present until he appeared part way through the next course and they came face to face. Brought so suddenly to mind of her dealings with him last night, she blushed.

And then something made her glance towards where Laura was seated at the foot of the table. Laura had seen her exchange with Austin and was sitting, perfectly still, her face contorted with – what?

Gillian blinked. Surely, logically, Laura should have been, if anything, pleased to see that she was on blushing terms with Austin – or indeed anyone other than Iain; should have been excited even, by the possibilities; should have been hoping that Iain too had registered Austin's special smile and Gillian's blush. (Which he had.)

But no. It was jealousy coming from Laura like daggers that Gillian could feel; jealousy so powerful and blatant that everyone else in that room could hardly fail to be aware of it too.

Slowly Gillian's gaze was drawn to the man sitting next to Laura. Time stood still as they regarded each other.

And now Laura had intercepted *that* look and was glaring angrily at Iain – an anger that was hastily concealed when he turned to look at her.

Feeling that the cross-currents were becoming quite unbearable, Gillian left the kitchen for a few minutes. She went into the cool old dairy and opened the freezer chest. She leaned downwards, appreciating the cold air, and poked noisily about among the grouse, shot by her cousin Richard on the Glorious Twelfth.

It was ironic really, she thought. She had been so revolted that night at the Grange when Terry Dunlop had told her about the television interviewer asking Iain if the fact that Giles Falconer had two pretty daughters had influenced him in his decision to come here. And now – look at the influence he was having on them! He had been here only twelve days but already one daughter was hell-bent on marrying him at all costs. And the other…

For all anyone knew, she thought, as she rearranged the frozen bundles into a pyramid, the last thing that Iain might have in mind at the moment was a deep and committed relationship with *anyone*. For all anyone knew he might have no intention of staying around once he was fit again and the mill on its feet. Perhaps he was glad of Laura's skills, and now hers, for the benefit of the mill and glad of their friendliness (if that was the right word) for the benefit of himself – as recuperational therapy. The packages slithered suddenly down in all directions.

Someday, she vowed, she would learn to live with the pain of loving him. She brought the lid down with controlled violence as fighting spirit flooded her veins. In the meantime, she'd recuperational therapy him! Just let anyone, *anyone*, get the impression that she was in any way shape or form a languishing lovelorn maiden. Head held high she marched back into the kitchen.

Instead of resuming her neglected duties Gillian deliberately seated herself next to Austin. He turned quickly to her, catching her mood.

'Are you going shooting tonight?' he asked in a low intimate voice, too low for the others to hear, letting her know what subject Reg had introduced to bring the atmosphere down to normal in her absence.

'I might. I just might,' Gillian replied quite audibly.

'What are you two whispering about?' demanded Laura.

'Not whispering, Laura.'

Only now did it occur to her that after Saturday's demonic outburst there should be a certain restraint to say the least between Laura and herself. But this did not seem to be so. She waited to see what Laura would say next, the new light that kept confounding her sister back in her eyes.

'What were you talking about then?'

'The same as you: shooting.' She looked Laura speculatively up and down as if choosing which part of her she might aim a gun at, a look of bland good humour on her face, secretly marvelling at her own performance.

One last smile into those ready bright blue eyes beside her and she slid out of her seat to go over to Brian, who was carving the remains of a turkey for the second sitting, due to arrive at any moment. Brian stopped work as she approached and stood looming anxiously over her, the wicked-looking knife in his hand.

'That's lovely, Brian,' she said, smiling up at him. 'Did your father teach you to carve?'

'Mum,' he mumbled, grinning fatuously down at her.

The others appeared to be unable to take their eyes off her. Reg's held an unholy glint of amusement.

Gillian removed hot plates from the range, took bread sauce, stuffing and other good things from their warm places. Christine and Liz appeared. The kitchen resumed its normal tempo.

'We must fly, Iain. That was the whole point of coming early. We must see all these people this afternoon.' Laura took Iain's hand and began to drag him across the kitchen, taking the trouble to make a charming picture of this somewhat juvenile act.

That was *twice* that Iain's hand had been allowed to touch Laura's female flesh Gillian did not fail to note. She could feel Iain trying to catch her eye as they passed her but she was too busy making an unnecessarily thorough job of rinsing out a pan to do more than glance at him. To his 'see you, Gillian,' she responded with only the briefest and most nonchalant of murmurs.

As the jeep left the yard Gillian let out a long breath then proceeded to become the life and soul of the kitchen, watched bodingly by Liz. Liz's radar had picked something up the instant she came through the door. Since then she had been sniffing the air intently; had absorbed every nuance of Laura and Iain's exit.

The whole affair, she now concluded, had taken another turn for the even messier. What to do about it though? Clearly a sharp push somewhere was badly needed to get the thing running properly. But how and where to administer it? She would have to think of something – quickly.

*****

Later on that afternoon, during a lull, Liz picked up the tackroom extension and rang her father's scrapyard. After some delay Richard was located and came to the phone. No, he said, he didn't want to go to the clay pigeon shoot. He was tired and intended to have an early night.

Being less than a year older than Liz (his sister) and Gillian, Richard had shared their baby and toddlerhood, their early school years and, on and off, their lives generally ever since.

Gillian had not seriously considered going to the shoot. She was, however, thinking sour thoughts about the others going instead of getting on with her drawing when the low, rakish sports car that Richard had built himself reversed up Church Row and stopped at her door.

Something about the sulky way he worded his invitation made it, for some reason, irresistible.

'Yes, dammit. I'll come,' she said through gritted teeth. She ran upstairs and very quickly got changed.

'What are you wearing that thing for?' he greeted her reappearance with, looking with disfavour at the red butcherboy cap that went with her newly taken-in trouser suit.

'To keep my head warm,' she replied looking critically at the loud checked cap he had not bothered to remove.

'It'll keep what few brains you've got intact, I suppose,' he said grudgingly.

Normal relations thus established, the car hurtled past the neighbouring cottages, not with the roar one would expect from the car's rakish appearance, but with the wholly satisfying sound of the perfectly tuned Rolls Royce engine concealed beneath its long, long bonnet.

Richard soon embarked on a detailed complaint about the way the planners were wrecking the economy, his favourite subject. Gillian elected to say yes and no in all the right places with exaggerated insincerity until he told her to shut up. A pheasant scuttling up a bank out of their path, its hen following, gave his thoughts a different turn. Poaching was his main pursuit outside working hours.

'It's nearly dark,' Gillian reminded him as he slowed the car down and seemed to be looking for a place to stop.

'It wouldn't have taken a minute,' he said in an ill-used voice.

The car picked up speed again and very soon they were in the car park of the pub where the shoots were held. They could see Laura from where they were parked. She was taking aim; Iain stood at her shoulder.

'Miss!' prayed Gillian.

Laura missed. Richard eyed his cousin sideways and strolled off, their guns under his arm, to where he had spotted Reg, Liz and the vicar. Liz greeted Gillian like a long lost sister and totally ignored her brother.

After that they both put on a great display of enjoying themselves very much until the twilight deepened into moonlight and it was finally time to call a halt.

A friendly spaniel greeted them as they entered the pub. They parted naturally into two groups, Laura and Iain with Austin and the vicar forming one group at a table. The others went to sit at the bar.

The next hour passed very quickly indeed, or so it seemed to Gillian. Occasionally she threw a laughing glance at the nearby table. The vicar appeared to be holding forth non-stop every time she looked and Iain was listening to him. Laura's expression became darker and darker until Austin suddenly changed seats and sat down next to her. Laura straightened as if shot. Slowly she turned to him, her face grim and intent.

Sometime before closing time they all left the pub, Richard somehow spiriting Gillian out ahead of the others. They were well on the road before the others had squeezed themselves into the army vehicle and the other cars they had come in.

'Why are you stopping?' asked Gillian, as Richard drew the car off the road and parked on a small headland overlooking a disused quarry.

'To make violent love to you of course,' replied Richard sarcastically. 'Why else do people stop in secluded places in the middle of the night?' He wound his window down.

'I wouldn't call this secluded,' argued Gillian. 'Exposed I'd call it.'

'Shut up will you. I'm trying to listen.'

'What to? A pheasant, I suppose, or whatever it is you go after at night.'

'I never did like you.'

'So why are you kissing me?'

'Liz said I'd got to.'

She tried to struggle free. He kissed her again, holding her distinctively shaped cap in place when it became in danger of being dislodged. Their silhouette must have been quite unmistakable in the blinding beams of the vehicle coming up behind them. Gillian recognised the engine note as it roared by. Richard stopped kissing her and let her cap fall off. He kept his arm around her though.

'She said to go on ahead. Park somewhere we can't miss seeing you, she said. Kiss her when we're going past…'

'She said,' Gillian finished for him. 'Since when have you done anything Liz told you to? Anyway they've gone now. She didn't tell you to put on a porn show, did she?' She removed his hand from where it had strayed. He immediately put it back. She removed it again. He put it back.

'They've gone now,' she repeated.

'I must be tireder than I thought. I quite fancy you just at this moment.'

'You can't possibly. It's – it's incestuous!'

'Oh – worse than that. I've always thought of you as a nasty little brother. I used to call you Mr Piggy. Remember? That was before you got thin. I quite like you thin.'

He kissed her again for several moments. She forgot to try and stop him, her thoughts with the occupants of the jeep. She would kill Liz when she saw her next. On the other hand – what better way of demonstrating that she was not a languishing maiden?

Richard's feelings were evidently deepening and, after a while, in an *academic* sort of way, she noticed that she was finding it mildly catching. Only very mildly, of course. Not quite sure how to handle this unexpected development she was quite glad when he suddenly got hiccups. She started copying his hiccups each time one came. And then she got the giggles. How many brandies had she had, she wondered?

'I'm going home now,' he said. 'I'm hungry and I'm tired.'

'You're always hungry. Why are you tired?'
'You'd be tired if you'd not been to bed since Sunday.'
'Where were you? Poaching, I suppose.'
'No I wasn't, clever clogs.' He started the car.
'Where were you then?' she asked as they swept along.
'Fetching a thing up from Cardiff. Police wouldn't let us do it in the daytime. Took all the road up.'
'That's millionaires,' said Gillian philosophically.
'I'm not a millionaire.'
'Have patience. You're only twenty three.'
'Fancy some chips?' was his only reply to this sally.
'Wait till I see Liz,' said Gillian, her thoughts returning to what the earlier scene must have looked like, lit up in the army vehicle's powerful headlights.
'Shall I catch 'em up for you?' He yawned again.
'No thanks. It'll keep.'

*****

The new Edwardian nightgown was waiting for her when shortly after midnight Gillian went upstairs to bed. Brenda must have collected it earlier from Beatrice and laid it out to greet her. It was quite delightful, more than fulfilling the vision Gillian had had in her mind when she sketched it.

She hurried out of her clothes and put it on. Its whisper-soft red folds caressed warmly about her. Lavish ivory lace trimmings glowed sumptuously as she surveyed herself in the long mirror on the wall.

A sharp double-rap on the front door interrupted her contemplation. Her green eyes meet those reflected ones above the ruched neckline in the mirror for a startled second. She turned and ran downstairs telling Jasper to be quiet and jerked open the door, keeping her nightdress-clad person discreetly out of sight behind it, although it was quite dark both outside and in.

Iain strode in briskly.

'In future, Gillian, put the chain on that door before you open it at night to *anyone*.'

'Major Hamp… You *touched* me!'

'And that's another thing: Iain, Gillian. Say Iain.'

He was a completely different man. Had she Liz to thank for this? Had he now decided she was a good old-fashioned woman of easy virtue and so…

The door was kicked shut and he had her back against the wall, her hands pinned on either side of her. The harsh feel of his palms sent a pang of unutterable pleasure through her.

'*Iain.*' His voice came threateningly down in the darkness. His body was pressing against hers. She could feel his immediate warmth through the fine material of her nightgown.

'I – Iain,' she gasped.

'Again!'

Sanity left her completely. 'Kiss me – Iain.'

'I intend to. I've got…'

He pulled her urgently away from the wall to get his arms around her. His mouth came down and all chance of reason fled. The kiss grew deeper and deeper. Unmindful of his damaged back she strained herself closer to him.

Then her fingers, curling up around his shoulders encountered the crowns. He released her slightly as she stiffened and uttered an inarticulate cry against his lips.

'You're in army things. *Why are you in uniform Iain…?*'

He raised his head, listening. She heard it too – the clatter of a helicopter coming nearer.

'I thought I'd have about ten minutes.' She was seized again, his embrace unbearably sweet now she realized it was fraught with imminent parting.

The clattering passed overhead, lessening slightly as the helicopter continued on its way to Falcon Park to wait for this man – tearing him away from her arms where he belonged only minutes, precious minutes after he had committed himself to them. And she to his.

'I don't know how long I'll be, my love. Could be months. We're going back.' He found the switch and flooded the room with sudden light so that he could have one last look at her.

He caught his breath at the sight of her in her nightgown, her face flushed with love, her green eyes huge with distress. His agony of mind expressed itself as his fist crashed against the overhead beam.

She laid her hands against his chest. 'Will it be as dreadful?'

'Not if the US Army can help it. When we've done what we've got to do we'll be getting Steve and Bernie back – if we can find where we buried them. That's why it could take months. Big place where we're going.'

She flung her arms around his neck as he snatched her close again in urgent farewell, telling her wordlessly by the way he held her what she needed so desperately to know.

The final lock gates, behind which she had forced herself to dam her love, opened. 'Iain, you know… You do know…'

But he would not let her finish. 'Not yet,' he silenced her, his lips against hers. 'We mustn't say these things. Not yet.'

There was a moment of stillness as they absorbed each other's unspoken declaration. Then he relaxed against her, his head on her shoulder.

'At two o'clock every afternoon think of me. Will you?'

'Oh Iain – I'll be thinking of you at two o'clock and three and four.'

'I'll work out the time differences. Around seven in the morning it will be. And I'll meet you there in space. Every day.'

'Two o'clock,' she whispered.

One long last kiss, then he was gone. She followed him out into the road, uncaring of the frosty air.

Others were out there too, most of them, like her, in their night clothes, drawn out by the racket of the helicopter. Brenda came tramping towards her in a voluminous blue dressing-gown. Together they strained their eyes to catch the fleeting glimpses in the uncertain moonlight of the figure running towards the menacing lights of the throbbing monster.

Gillian shuddered.

'Get in,' said Brenda roughly. 'I'll put the kettle on. You'll catch your death out here. We'll hear it when it takes off. You can come out and wave then.'

She pushed her indoors and closed the door behind them with a bang that reverberated through Gillian like the final clap of doom.

TWELVE

Gillian's parents were there to meet her when the luxury coach pulled in at Harrogate.

Victoria had to take a deep breath to rally her forces when her daughter came down the steps. Elizabeth had warned her of course, but… 'Yes, you have got nice and slim, haven't you love,' she said briskly by way of greeting. 'Elizabeth said you had and that it suited you.' She kissed Gillian. 'The car's over there, look.'

'Too thin.' Gillian's father came up behind them with Gillian's luggage. 'Is Liz not feeding you properly?'

'I'll say she is. Brenda too. I think it's their happy conditions. They both treat me like their lone chick. In shifts – Liz all day and Brenda all night.'

They put themselves and Gillian's suitcases into the Rolls Royce and Giles took the wheel.

'They'll no doubt abandon me in April when their real babies land,' Gillian added. 'I'll probably starve to death then for all they'll care. At the moment they're just practising.'

'Well you certainly look fighting fit,' her mother declared. 'What clothes have you brought?'

Gillian told her. Victoria recognised them all by their descriptions. They dated back to that other lifetime, before the massive loan from Hampshire Holdings; before she left her family to pursue its path to ruin, being herself unable to tolerate living on borrowed money, and went off into the unknown to carve a living for herself. And for Giles and Gillian when ruin came. (She had used her mother's legacy, which Giles had refused to touch, to buy the then almost derelict mansion. And Elizabeth had invested her share too.)

'But they are all size sixteen,' she pointed out. 'They'll fall off you.'

'They would've until Beatrice got at them. She's Victorianised them too, as per your orders. I didn't know you'd had snow!'

They discussed the snow and whether it would still be there tomorrow – Christmas Day. Gillian seemed cheerful enough to satisfy her father. Victoria, however, was not fooled for one moment. It had only taken that first sight of her daughter as she appeared in the doorway of the coach for her maternal radar to pick up the deep un-ease hidden beneath the tranquil outer skin.

However, being a firm believer in all things positive, she decided that Gillian's veneer of cheerfulness was a good thing. She reviewed all the most recent items of village and family gossip to reach her via Elizabeth's and Laura's weekly phone calls, and Gillian's letters, and was ready with the most interesting nugget.

And what's all this about Lance Drysdale inheriting three million from a batty old aunt provided he gets married within six months of her death?' she asked.

Gillian giggled and her mother congratulated herself. This was a promising start.

'Sounds like a load of moonshine to me,' observed Giles. 'But if it's true Laura could do a lot worse. They've been in and out of each other's pockets for years. He's a damned good auctioneer too.'

His ladies waited to hear what else he had to say. Gillian glanced at her watch. It was twenty minutes to two. Only once had she failed to keep her daily meeting across the ether with Iain and that had been one Sunday soon after he had gone when she had fallen asleep after lunch through sheer exhaustion. Those had been hectic days back in October and there had been no days off.

'But I suppose she's still hankering after that Hampshire chap,' Giles concluded.

'Soon be there,' said Victoria robustly, carefully not looking at Gillian. 'You'll like the new wing, Gillian. Your father's worked wonders.'

'Yes – you said in your letters that he'd charged in like the U.S. Cavalry,' responded Gillian, apparently untroubled by her father's last words.

'Did I?'

Giles was pretending not to listen.

'You did. And that he'd blitzed the Building Inspector, bulldozed the architect, stampeded the masons, terrorised the joiners. I forget what he did to the electricians. Oh!'

They had arrived. As if on cue, fat snowflakes began to fill the air.

'It's a fairytale Christmas card!'

'Yes, it is rather,' her mother agreed modestly.

The low-slung snow-clouds brought twilight to the early afternoon. Welcoming beams gleamed out from all the windows and the wide-open front door. A family was unloading itself and its trappings under the iron lace-hung portico assisted by a large and glowing young woman in Victorian costume, whose Canadian voice rang out cheerfully in the snowy air. She waved to the occupants of the Rolls drawn up beyond.

'That's Janni,' said Victoria. 'Shall we get out or have you not finished looking?'

'I could draw it for next year's Christmas card from the mill.'

'You could,' agreed her father, drily. 'Shall I go and get you some paper and crayons?'

Above the front door was a clock tower and, looking at it, Gillian realised with a start that the clock, old though it was, was telling the right time. She had about seven minutes somehow to find seclusion.

A fair-haired youth disguised as a Victorian footman detached himself from the mêlée in the hall and ran towards them. He was introduced to Gillian and allowed to take charge of her and her suitcases.

'Hi,' Janni called out as she ushered the last child in through the front door.

Gillian found herself in the large square hall, transformed since last she was there, with garlands and holly, a huge log fire roaring in the magnificent Victorian fireplace. The newly arrived family were being made to feel at home by two more footmen who were already loaded up with the larger suitcases and preparing to lead them to their rooms, with exhortations to come downstairs again as soon as they had changed into Victorian gear for drinks around the fire.

Gillian's footman, George, escorted her with gratifying enthusiasm to her room on the first floor next to her parent's suite at the back of the mansion. Much as he would have liked to linger to help her settle in, George had to leave her then as he was needed downstairs. More arrivals were expected at any minute.

What perfect timing! It was two minutes to two. Gillian sank down on the deep sprung bed, with its wealth of highly polished brass knobs at its head and foot, and closed her eyes.

There was no way of proving that this daily tryst in space was an actual happening, that Iain was there with her in mind during those exact minutes each day, but Gillian's faith that this was true was so strong it did not need proof. Her sureness that they were communicating in spirit was her strength during his physical absence.

And strength was needed as not one word of news had there been since the night in September when that helicopter snatched him away, which was very hard to bear. From time to time Daniel would let it be known that he had rung headquarters and each time been informed that next-of-kin would be informed in certain events. So presumably the men were, so far at least, considered to be not missing.

Today, as she concentrated, Gillian received a distinct extra feeling. This had happened before sometimes but not very often, as though the mood Iain was in was managing to reach her across the thousands of miles that separated them. Here, in these new surroundings, she felt certain that Iain was at that moment laughing about something. Her lips curved into an answering smile.

There was something else too. She listened intently to her extra sensory perceptions, not letting her imagination provide messages of its own. There seemed to be no message, so what was it?

She held her breath and waited. And then it came to her like a thunderclap. Iain was closer today – much closer.

She jumped to her feet. She must get back to Great Bowland somehow, immediately. She should have obeyed her instincts and stayed at home; should have known that the expedition would have aimed to get home for Christmas. Somehow she must borrow or hire a car from somewhere. Would Janni help her?

A tap came at the door and Janni appeared.

'Ah! Just the…'

But Janni knew a person poised for flight when she saw one.

'Honey, you've still got your coat on. Come on – I'll unpack for you.'

'No – I…'

Janni opened one of the cases and lifted out a long brown heavily braided velvet skirt. She exclaimed delightedly as she held it up; then she laid it down on the bed. Soon all the other garments were spread out there too and Janni began putting them on hangers, keeping up a flow of words about how Giles and Victoria were over the moon about having their long lost daughter for Christmas – the ultimate Christmas present. She asked about Gillian's journey and before she could answer mentioned that she had just heard on the local radio that the road over the Blubberhouse Moors was now impassable due to freezing fog, which must have come down almost as soon as Gillian's coach got through.

The need to get back home was still driving Gillian but Janni was getting through to her. No – she could not turn tail and bolt she realised. Not after all the trouble everyone had gone to to persuade her to take this break. She must soldier on. She had kept vigil patiently for three long months and must go on doing so. If Iain was back in the country he would soon contact her – even if the Pennines were impassable. If she could just hear his voice…

And it was always possible that her telepathy had got it wrong, in which case everyone would think she had gone mad if she went back before her five day holiday had started. It had taken quite a lot of persuasion to uproot her in the first place as her work was her lifeline. She needed to be occupied every minute of every day as that was the only way the awful waiting, waiting, could be borne. She had welcomed all the pressures and challenges. It was the others who had decreed that she had overdone things and must take this rest with her overjoyed parents; must have a change of scene.

Liz had threatened to sack her if she did not go and had gone to some lengths to demonstrate that she was now at last feeling supremely fit all day long, it being the fifth month. (How appalled Liz had been in the earlier months to discover that pregnancy was going to lay her, of all people, so low in the mornings!)

And Christine had assured her, in confidence, that she was prepared to put up with Austin helping her full time for the five days, seeing he'd volunteered and seeing he'd got all his ewes down to the fields close to the farm on purpose so he could keep an eye on them at the same time as doing Gillian's job in the stables.

This had made Gillian smile for several reasons and finally decided her. Austin deserved a break and she had reason to want to help him. Christine was giving him a very hard time and she, inevitably, it was – the only woman in the whole valley known to be impervious to his charms – who Austin had decided was the one woman he wanted to marry and settle down with.

He needed all the help he could get, what with having to prove that at last he truly was a reformed rake and had sown all his wild oats, plus the struggle he was having, trying to overcome the steady loathing for him that Christine had had, for some undisclosed reason, since early childhood. The idea of leaving the two of them to run the stables without her had struck Gillian as being rather a good one.

Aunt Elizabeth too had urged Gillian to come away; had undertaken to help Liz feed the men; had booked her seat on the coach when at last she consented and, this morning, driven her in to Clitheroe to catch it.

As for Laura – Laura had *ordered* her to come. The Bowland Forest Range was well in hand now. Laura wanted Gillian to have a break and come back fresh and ready to embark on the designing of a second series.

Slowly Gillian began to undo the many buttons of her new Cossack coat. Laura. At least if she stopped here she would not lay eyes on Laura for a few days.

Janni whisked the matching fur hat off her head and found a place for it in the wardrobe, still talking all the time, about the programme for the next few days and the help she could do with, keeping kids out of adult hair; about the carol singing they were relying on Gillian to play the piano for; about the piano itself – a Victorian find Giles had bought only last week and had had tuned.

Gillian took off her coat and with it shrugged off her backward-looking thoughts. Janni was twinkling at her, scenting her change of mood and holding out a padded coat-hanger. She could return to her reception desk now, confident that Gillian would shortly appear among them looking as stunning as her stunning mother, in the gorgeous brown velvet skirt and complicated ivory blouse she had left out on the bed.

A small band of children watched Gillian as she came downstairs. Seeing them, she turned herself into a Hollywood screen goddess, making an entrance for their benefit. The regal smile on her face changed when she reached them into quite a different smile, which turned her into their instant playmate. They bore her off to help with the Christmas trees, thoughtfully left for them to decorate.

*****

The days flashed by and each day at two o'clock Iain's presence felt closer and closer. Gillian was convinced that the Atlantic and half a continent no longer separated them. If his mission was ended he would find a way to contact her. Surely he would!

But as the days passed by and he felt nearer and closer, doubt began to stir. Especially in the darkness of the night watches. So strong was the feeling that he was close enough to contact her that, for the first time, the unthinkable began to insinuate itself in her mind.

Meanwhile, her mother was delicately trying to discover for herself exactly how things stood. She knew from Elizabeth all that was generally known about Iain's twelve days in Great Bowland and had heard even more about it from Laura. But she also knew that Iain had kept the helicopter waiting while he paid a last visit to Gillian's cottage. Everyone knew about that because neighbours had been out there when he left the cottage that night and ran off like the wind to Falcon Park. The neighbours had seen Gillian out there too, wearing a red nightdress. But no one knew what had taken place at the cottage because no one, not even Liz, had managed to coax one word out of Gillian about it. So a great deal of guessing had been done instead.

Watching Gillian as day followed day, Victoria grew certain that Liz's theory was correct and that some kind of commitment had been made that night between Gillian and Iain. But what of Laura?

Gillian was, naturally, very close and dear to her mother. But so too was Laura close and dear to her, and she to Laura. And Laura was adamant that *she* was going to marry Iain, that nothing and nobody was going to stop her.

Victoria's delicate probing usually took the form of bolt-from-the-blue questions. She fired off one of these on Boxing Day after they got back from a matinée performance of Aladdin in Harrogate, when everyone was changing back into nineteenth century dress again.

'And what's all this about Laura and Austin?' she called through the open door between their bedrooms.

A thoughtful silence seemed to be the only response. What indeed about Laura and Austin! Gillian was not surprised her mother had heard about it. What had been surprising – more than surprising – was Laura's failure to keep the whole thing secret.

From the day following Iain's departure Laura had relentlessly worn the cloak, not only of queen-bloody-beehood (Liz's description), but of wife-apparenthood too. That it was only a question of time before she became the wife of the head of Hampshire Holdings was something Laura was at great pains to allow no one, and in particular Gillian, to forget.

And yet, within a week of Iain's going, when Austin moved in for the kill, Laura, incredibly, had allowed herself to be beguiled. Even more incredibly, even after the news of their affaire had flashed through the valley, Laura had continued to behave as though her right to marry Iain when he came back still had full validity!

Laura's amorality had been one of Gillian's main comforts, because there had been times when she so admired Laura and what she was achieving at the mill that she had felt pangs of regret, almost, that she was going to be the one to deprive Laura of what she still evidently considered to be her certain reward and destiny.

It helped Gillian a lot to know about Laura's public fling with Austin. Here was proof that she was not capable of fidelity and was not, therefore, in any way worthy of marriage to a man like Iain.

Victoria appeared suddenly in the doorway, still not fully dressed.

'Liz told Elizabeth that Laura took to coming to the farm without any excuse and not in the Porsche. Liz said the Peugeot was a lot roomier and would convert into a passion-wagon at the flick of a knob or two.'

'And if your guests only knew you were wearing *that* under all that goody-goody…'

'And Liz said Austin went galloping off up the fell and Blackie landed back without him half an hour later.'

'Which was a black lie! Blackie would never come home without Austin. It was Dark Knight. Liz must be losing her grip completely if she thought it was Blackie, even if they are identical.'

Which told Victoria that Gillian was glad about Laura's lapse but was not going to tell tales to Mother. Her loyalty was quite wasted of course because she had no illusions about the child she had reared and loved as her own: Jessica Hall's child. Most of the Halls were amoral, including Jessica. Good at running Falcon Mill and all that, but takers – jealous, feuding, possessive, amoral takers.

Her Rottweiler shouldered his way past the billows of her underskirt and went to talk to Gillian. She tickled him behind one ear and waited to see what bolt the figure in the black lace corselette and the long crimson skirt in the doorway would fire next from her crossbow.

But all Victoria said, as if to herself, was: 'They'll deal very well together.'

'And three million is not to be sniffed at,' added Gillian, as if to Cassius.

Victoria turned thoughtfully away. She had, of course, been referring to Laura and Lance Drysdale, not Laura and Austin, as anyone listening might have assumed. Gillian's quickness, her divining whom she meant, was almost telepathic.

The thought made Victoria pause on her way to her dressing room. She was herself no stranger to telepathy, having a strong link with Elizabeth, which was not unusual between twins. Had Gillian discovered its power too?

Suddenly Victoria knew that she had – it explained why Gillian grew restless then disappeared sometime after lunch. Even today at the theatre she had managed to go missing at about – when? About two o'clock was it? Yes – two o'clock must be the time appointed. But what was the explanation for the uneasiness she could sense growing daily in Gillian? Was something upsetting getting through to her by telepathy – or by breakdown of telepathy – from Iain Hampshire?

There was not really time now to speculate. In the meantime, although yes, Laura and Lance Drysdale probably would deal very well together someday (quite soon if the aunt's deadline was to be met), Gillian's path was still far from smooth. Nor was it strewn with roses.

As if to confirm that she could indeed read thoughts, Gillian's voice followed her as she went into the dressing room beyond her bedroom.

'Laura's probably at this moment working out how to set up a ménage á trois.'

*****

On the fifth and final day, if Gillian had wanted proof that all her daily meetings in space so far had taken place, proof came. At two o'clock, as she sat in her room concentrating, *Iain was not there.* She waited twenty minutes. Nothing happened.

*****

The snow had been short-lived and in the ensuing slush Giles decided that he and Gillian should take that walk they had been promising themselves since Gillian arrived on Christmas Eve. This was her last day. She would be off on the tea-time coach, if coaches were still running. Her father found her in her room, not getting on with her packing.

Already the slush was freezing into crisp peaks and channels that crunched beneath their wellingtons. Cassius bounded ahead. Numb and distracted Gillian let her father's pleasant voice wash over her, taking in about one word in five. He was telling her about Daniel who had appeared at Old Hall one weekend.

At first they had not known he worked for Hampshire Holdings. 'He booked in for the weekend,' Giles told Gillian. 'The alterations were at a tricky stage then. Chaos everywhere. We knew we were on the right lines and everything was going to blend in. But the planners were being such a confounded nuisance we were having to compromise with one damned thing and another to the extent we knew we were going to end up with something less stylish than we were aiming for. Then this chap wandered in.'

Gillian forced her mind to work, forced herself to sound calm and interested. She fixed a picture in her mind of the new conservatory. The effort was superhuman.

'And you didn't notice him much at first,' she produced. 'And now you've got that utterly splendid conservatory off the new wing that not even the planners could veto. He's a genie.' She went on, gaining strength from somewhere. 'They call him That Daniel in the village. Everyone has a tale to tell about him. They've a huge new gate at the farm in the wall opposite one of the milking parlours where no way through ever was before. It saves miles. Daniel moved the first stone.'

The genie had caused other things to happen too but Gillian could not talk about them. He had closed Falcon Park and vanished. He had reappeared with Iain's clothes, spirited away from Marianna Merrivale (now Parker). These he had left with Mrs. Appleton who had washed or cleaned them all lovingly before putting them carefully away in her spare bedroom.

Laura had heard about this and gone immediately to demand them. She had come up against a stone wall. Mrs. Appleton had never liked Laura and belonged to the half of the village that considered Gillian, not Laura, the rightful bride of Falcon Park.

Mrs. Appleton had not invited Gillian to come and help her with Iain's clothes because she judged, rightly, that this would upset her as if going through the belongings of someone dead. Gillian had already been upset enough, although no one knew this, by catching sight of Iain's jeep passing in front of her along the main road as she cycled down Church Row on her way back to work one afternoon in October. For a few seconds her heart had stopped beating altogether during which she saw that it, and the car behind it, had uniformed strangers at their wheels.

The rest of the walk was taken up with detailed enquiries about the reorganisation of the canteen at the mill which had been re-christened the Dining Hall since Gillian and Laura had made it so attractive.

'And how the Dickens you found time I don't know,' Giles remarked. 'When did you get all that drawing done?'

'After dark mostly,' admitted Gillian. 'I got all the masters off before the end of November. They more or less drew themselves once I got into the vein. I don't know when stuff'll start to appear in the shops. They're printing it at Pontefract until the new machines at the mill start work, which should be any minute now.'

'Laura's certainly been lashing everyone along,' he observed cheerfully. He was well-contented with his new life and never brooded about might-have-beens concerning his family's old mill. 'Actually – your stuff might not be in the shops yet but some of it will be at Old Hall before the end of the week. Daniel's getting us a consignment – wallpaper as well. We're going to do one of the new suites out completely in Gillian Falconer designs. We're going to call it the Gillian Suite.'

They arrived back at Old hall just before four o'clock and Gillian went straight up to finish packing. Now she was alone again her distress all at once became quite unbearable. She lay down on the bed, fighting panic; telling herself she was over-reacting and letting her imagination run away with her. After all, she herself had failed to keep tryst with Iain that Sunday when she fell asleep. Perhaps today he had fallen asleep. Or…

Abruptly she rolled off the bed, wrenched down her suitcases from the top of the wardrobe and flung them on the bed, wrestling with the out-of-control monsters in her head that were suggesting, suggesting. Having tumbled in all her clothes, she fumbled among the odds and ends on her bedside table and knocked something off. It was a remote control. As she picked it up she unintentionally pressed one of the buttons. The television sprang to life behind her.

*****

On the floor below Victoria moved from room to room. Some guests had departed and others, here for New Year, were finding their way about. All the televisions in the public rooms seemed to be switched on to the same channel. Preoccupied as she was with the frustration of being unable to do anything about the burdens her child was carrying, Victoria took no notice of the first two screens she walked past.

At the third set she paused. A dim chord from the past was sounding in her memory. She stood watching for a few moments. Yes, she had seen it many years ago. It was a short story. Was it by Somerset Maugham? Someone like that, and it had an upsetting ending. She moved into one of the bars trying to recall what was so upsetting about it.

From what she remembered it was the tale of an impoverished young couple who fell in love and were trying to save up enough money to marry. But the young man, a postman, was tempted and stole money from the mail and received a prison sentence. The girl spent the time he was locked up living for the day they would be together again and scrimping and slaving to get a couple of rooms somewhere ready for when that time came.

But, Victoria recalled, on the eve of his release, the young man found that his violent love for the girl had burnt out with its own over-intensity and all he knew now was that he had so sickened himself of thinking about her that he never wanted to see her again.

So a message was sent to the girl who, having nothing to live for any more, committed suicide.

Victoria left the bar abruptly. Gillian did not watch television normally but there was just a chance she had decided to switch on the set in her room while she was packing. There were enough uncertainties making Gillian thin and haunted without putting those sorts of possibilities into her head as well.

Her mother ran upstairs and along the corridor to Gillian's room. One of the other bedroom doors was open and she caught a glimpse of the screen in there as she hurried past. Was everyone in the hotel watching this thing? The glimpse was enough to tell her that the girl had received the blow. She was too late. In the few seconds it took to reach Gillian's door she prayed that the screen inside would be blank.

It was, but the remote control was there in Gillian's hand. Her mother took a deep breath.

'You've not been watching that miserable old thing?' she asked briskly, as if the look on Gillian's face had not already confirmed it. 'I saw it thirty-odd years ago. I felt like kicking the screen in. Was the non-hero that man who was in that lion thing and that lovely lovely film *Geordie*? Have you finished? Shall I sit on them – or you can. I'll do up the clasps. Come and have a drink – we've half an hour or so.' She carried on talking as she led the way down to the bar, carrying Gillian's larger case.

In the car a short while later Victoria said to her: 'Anyway – don't forget, love, there's a home and a job waiting for you here once you've seen Liz through.'

'We're thinking of getting a few ponies and so on,' put in Giles.

'Don't worry Mum. I'll not commit suicide. I'd marry Richard first. Anyway, I haven't got a gas oven.'

This effectively took her mother's breath away but her father had only heard one word.

'*Suicide!* What's this?'

'No one's going to commit suicide, Dad. Forget that story, Mum.'

But will you? asked Victoria silently. She closed her eyes and sent a telepathic message to her twin. *Be there for her, Elizabeth, if the worst comes to the worst.*

*****

Victoria was right of course. The tale was in full possession of Gillian's mind. It was an eerie ride home. The coach rocked with steady purpose through the icy gloom of the moonlit Pennines, carrying her in overheated comfort to God alone knew what. She felt isolated from the other passengers and the real world. The security of Iain's love that had sustained her so far was disintegrating with every passing mile.

Of all the terrible ways of losing Iain himself that her imagination had provided, this was the one way that had never occurred to her. That his feelings for her had been so powerful that they could reach her from half a world away she had never doubted. That they could destroy themselves with their own power was something she would never have dreamed of – until that story suggested it to her.

The headlights of the coach picked up a sign by the road. LANCASHIRE, it said. It was only a road sign. She feared she had received a far more fundamental sign of things to come. The notion took obsessive root. She was *meant* to have that forewarning. She almost never watched television at home and yet her finger had pressed that button quite unintentionally, *automatically*, at that exact moment. It was a warning.

She had armed herself against the possibility that Iain could get killed. She had forced herself to do that. But against the chance that his love for her could have killed itself she had no armour at all.

And she knew exactly how the girl in the story felt.

*****

By arrangement the coach stopped before Clitheroe was reached so that she could get off and be picked up at a convenient layby by Liz, or someone detailed by her. The driver took her hand, guiding her cherishingly down the steps. The frozen air outside smote her but she scarcely noticed. He hauled out her suitcases and stood for a few moments, enquiring in a fatherly way if she was sure she was being met. It was pitch dark.

'Yes thank you,' she murmured.

'We're a few minutes early,' remarked the driver, riveted by the tragedy in her beautiful thickly-fringed eyes, unwilling to abandon her, despite the row of critical faces looking down on them through the windows of the coach.

As he spoke, Richard's long low car snaked into view and drew up ahead of the coach. The driver nodded approvingly, picking up her cases again. Like an automaton Gillian followed him. Richard already had the boot lid up.

Moments later they were away, whirling through the deserted icy lanes. Gillian made an effort after a mile or so and said: 'You're going too fast.'

'Stop nagging,' her cousin responded. The car slewed sideways around a wide corner, got back onto course and flew on to the next bend.

'Any news?' asked Gillian, still struggling to adjust to the here and now.

'Me mum's got flu.'

'Oh dear. Who's looking after her?'

'We are of course.'

'Poor Aunt Elizabeth. She'll not want the bug to get to Liz.'

'I'll not come in,' said Richard when they reached her door. 'There's smoke coming out of both your chimneys. She'll have the red carpet out no doubt. Good old Bren!'

'Thank you for the lift, dear Richard. I appreciate it.' She kissed him lightly.

He pulled a face at her and again told her to stop nagging. 'And don't slam that door.' As if she would.

At the last minute he seized hold of her and kissed her comprehensively.

'May as well make hay. That chap's back you know. Your hat tickles. Your Laura's chasing him up hill and down dale. Stupid bat!' He leapt out of the car and retrieved her luggage.

He drove away, leaving her rigid, standing by her suitcases. The door opened.

'He got you back in one piece then,' was Brenda's greeting. She took hold of a suitcase and went back indoors leaving the hysterics of reunion to Jasper. Gillian still stood.

'Told you, has he?' Brenda said, coming out again for the other suitcase, and for Gillian. 'Kettle's on.'

Gillian stood, her back to the fire, staring at Brenda, a score of questions unasked.

'Are you stopping – or what?' asked Brenda, indicating Gillian's coat.

Gillian sat down to remove her boots. Yes, she was stopping. She wasn't going to move an inch.

Brenda was looking wooden, which meant that she was worried. She was not one to beat about the bush, however, and in a few unvarnished words, as she hauled Gillian's long narrow boots off her, she let her know that Iain had been delivered to Mrs. Appleton's door by taxi the night before last.

He had been into the salon early yesterday morning for a trim during which he had been told where Gillian was, in case he didn't already know, which of course he did, from Mrs. Appleton. Laura had collected him from the salon and they had gone off somewhere, Iain driving.

All she, Brenda, had got out of him was that the tax on the Granada had run out and Daniel was doing something about it and that once he was back on four wheels he was off to Knutsford. 'Which is fair enough,' she allowed, as she moved into the kitchen to see to the tea things. 'His mum'll be needing to see him, no doubt.'

There was a pause as the teapot was heard being filled. 'He's not been seen since,' Brenda concluded flatly.

*****

The rest of the evening passed somehow. They drank tea, unpacked the suitcases. Brenda told her everything that had happened in the area during the past five days. Jasper sat on Gillian's feet whenever possible and kept within inches of her when not. Gillian responded stiltedly to all Brenda's news. She even managed to force down half a toasted scone.

Finally Brenda took herself off home and Gillian went upstairs to bed, allowing Jasper to come up with her just this once, although he was not normally supposed to go upstairs at all.

It was most unlikely, she felt, that she would sleep but it was vital to keep pretending to go through the motions of normality. She lay on her side watching the flames in the small hearth silhouetting Jasper as he lay before it, chin on paws, blissfully happy to be allowed to remain with his long-lost mistress.

Long before the last flame subsided into dust she fell into the deep sleep of emotional exhaustion, knowing nothing until first light.

THIRTEEN

At first she thought she was still dreaming in the confusion of noise that woke her. Jasper was barking in her ear and outside the window hoofs could be heard, clattering about in the near-darkness below.

She acknowledged that she was awake and forced herself to walk calmly to the window. It would be Munro, of course. He would be the chosen messenger and was going to take her for a ride while she got used to the news he brought.

The face below was indeed black. It only took the one quick glance she allowed herself to confirm that. In slow motion she went into the bathroom and then the other bedroom. She found a pair of thick stretch ski-pants and a warm Fairisle sweater, pulled on boots and rummaged along the rails for a long sheepskin jacket she used to wear when she was about fourteen, before she blossomed into her later curves.

Her helmet on, she was ready for the guillotine.

Jasper stormed out ahead of her and the horses threw up their heads. Clouds of steam from their snorting nostrils blew about the head of the tall man standing between them.

But the man was not Munro. The lower part of his face was hidden beneath a close black beard, but the upper part, she could now see in the dim dawn light, was dark brown, not black. Neither of them spoke.

Jasper and Bridgenorth had identified each other. The horse lowered his head and blew steam all over the dog.

The stranger let go the reins, came to attention and gave Gillian a full military salute. There was a moment of unreal stillness. Even the animals froze, their instincts catching the moment.

Then he became very active. He manoeuvred Bridgenorth away from the other hunter to make room for Gillian to mount. He turned to her and bowed deeply. Mesmerized, she moved towards him. She put her foot into

the hand held out ready for it and he sent her flying up into the saddle. She landed like a rag doll. He placed her foot in the stirrup and laced the reins meticulously through the fingers of her gloved hands.

Jasper could not believe his luck when the front door of the cottage was closed with him still outside it. He was going with them! Curtains twitched as they clattered down the terrace. They rode through the village and away in the direction of the Druid's Circle. And still not a word had been exchanged.

Sometimes he fell slightly behind and she could feel him looking at her. And sometimes he drew ahead and she could look her fill at him. His hair had grown quite long – thick and slightly curly. Brenda could not have trimmed all that much off. Gillian's tense lips relaxed into a smile. How typical of Brenda to keep the news of his beard to herself and let it be a surprise. How could he stand the cold on his bare head, his ears, after the steamy heat of the jungle?

He was a different being from the gaunt creature who came to the village to recover his health and strength those few months ago. His shoulders looked huge, even allowing for the bulk of the two thick sweaters he was wearing. His back was even straighter than before, his now well-filled muscles moved easily with the movements of the towering horse he was handling with silken assurance.

It all quite took her breath away.

A shout from a clump of trees on their left caused all five heads to turn towards the sound. Iain drew rein and Bridgenorth stopped too. After a further shout from the trees they went at a trot to investigate. As they neared the trees Munro appeared and limped towards them.

'Sprain?' called out Iain.

'Feels like it.'

Iain dismounted, handing Barney's reins to Gillian. It was now daylight. She looked disbelievingly down into the more than handsome face turned up to hers, the brilliant depths in his eyes holding hers for a searing moment.

Then he was down on one knee examining Munro's ankle and foot, Jasper skirmishing about, delighted with this fresh excitement. Bridgenorth recognised his former friend and moved forward, whickering. Munro spoke to him and stroked his nose, supporting himself with an arm on his neck while he raised his foot and cautiously turned it from side to side.

Nothing broken anyway,' decided Iain. 'Bar the odd ligament perhaps. Can you manage if we get you up on one of these?'

'No problem. You finish your ride – I'll get him back to the stables after I've got this strapped up.' He regarded them blandly as they looked at each other, the idea of sharing Bridgenorth's saddle taking root.

Then Gillian looked sharply at Munro. *Was* there anything wrong with his ankle? He was the most sure-footed person that she had ever met. Or was he engineering all this? Was Iain in on it too? Had *he* arranged it?

She was going to go along with it anyway. There was nothing more certain than that.

She watched with interest as Iain heaved him up into Barney's saddle. Munro crossed the stirrups in front of him and circled around them as Iain removed Gillian's foot from its stirrup, put his own foot in it and got himself up behind her with one powerful movement. Bridgenorth grunted as he adjusted himself to the extra weight.

And then they were off – one rider in the direction of the Grange, the other two heading in the general direction of Gracemire Farm, but not by the most direct route. His legs felt like iron. He had acquired her other stirrup now and, the leathers being a little short for him, his knees were bent so that her legs were supported in front of his along all their length.

'You can drive,' he said, his lips by her ear. His voice was soft and very deep.

A frisson shook her at these, the first words he had spoken to her. She took the reins from him with her gloved fingers, wishing she had not bothered to put them on, bitterly cold though it was.

Iain's hands were evidently cold too, because he put his right one, with some difficulty, in the pocket of his trousers. Next moment she discovered just how cold, as the left one slid inside the front of her jacket between its two buttons. The shock, even through the layer of thick wool, made her exclaim. Then an amazing warmth began to flow from that cold hand at her waist, which spread rapidly all over her body from the tips of her ears to the end of her toes in their fur-lined boots.

After that Bridgenorth plodded on unguided. He took the next turning on the left, lengthening his stride slightly, his nose now pointing in the direction of his warm stable. He contemplated breaking into a trot then thought better of it. His cargo felt secure enough but signals were no longer reaching him along the reins. So on he clopped at his fastest walk.

Eventually Iain spoke again. 'Where were you, Gillian, that Sunday? Were you asleep?'

At last she could trust her voice. 'I didn't mean to fall asleep. Where were you yesterday?'

'I was talking to Laura.'

Bridgenorth carried them several wordless yards before Iain continued: 'She phoned me. I was at my sister's. She wanted my advice.'

'Did you give it?' enquired Gillian politely.

'I wished her every possible happiness. I tried to think my way through to you when she rang off but it was no good. You seemed to be thinking about Daniel, not me. And greenhouses.'

It was uncanny. 'Conservatories, actually.' Gillian drew an excited breath. 'What am I thinking about now?'

He thought for a moment and then laughed. He hunched forward his shoulders, pressing them over hers so that he was moulded round her back like a shell.

'You're thinking that this is exactly what it's like being a tortoise.'

A delighted laugh shook her, the unspoken admission between them that at long last here he was, in his proper place: her shell; her home!

The deep voice spoke again by her ear. 'I love you Gillian.'

Gillian closed her eyes. Draping the reins over Bridgenorth's withers she abandoned them there. She reached up and removed her helmet.

'What did you say?' she whispered.

He tried the other ear, kissing it first. 'Gillian – I love you.' His lips returned to the first ear. 'I've left the army and I want to marry you. Could it be very soon?'

She tried to say something but found she couldn't. There was only one thing to do. It would be tricky, but she would manage it. Clutching her helmet strap and the buckle of the rains in one hand she twisted round. His hand being still it its warm place, his arm now encircled her completely. He turned the top half of his body to accommodate her, his other arm going urgently around her shoulders.

Their kiss lasted until the deserted stable buildings were reached.

'Will you?' he asked again, his lips a featherstroke away from hers.

She found her voice. 'I can't possibly not do.'

'Because?'

'Because,' she replied simply, 'I love you too.'